Parker Gillmore

Prairie Farms and Prairie Folk

Vol. II

Parker Gillmore

Prairie Farms and Prairie Folk
Vol. II

ISBN/EAN: 9783744772624

Printed in Europe, USA, Canada, Australia, Japan

Cover: Foto ©Andreas Hilbeck / pixelio.de

More available books at **www.hansebooks.com**

PRAIRIE FARMS

AND

PRAIRIE FOLK.

—

VOL II.

PRAIRIE FARMS

AND

PRAIRIE FOLK.

BY

PARKER GILLMORE,

("UBIQUE,")

AUTHOR OF "A HUNTER'S ADVENTURES IN THE GREAT WEST," ETC.

ON THE WABASH.

IN TWO VOLS.—VOL. II.

LONDON:

HURST AND BLACKETT, PUBLISHERS,

13, GREAT MARLBOROUGH STREET.

1872.

CONTENTS

OF

THE SECOND VOLUME.

CHAPTER I.

CHAPTER II.

CHAPTER III.

CHAPTER IV.

CHAPTER V.

CHAPTER VI.

CHAPTER VII.

CHAPTER VIII.

CHAPTER IX.

CHAPTER X.

CHAPTER XI.

CHAPTER XII.

CHAPTER XIII.

PRAIRIE FARMS AND PRAIRIE FOLK.

CHAPTER I.

Speculation in Coal Oil—"Sold" by a Secessionist—Ruffed Grouse—Prairie Chickens and American Partridge—Dangerous Sport—Pairing of Ruffed Grouse—Drumming—Appearance of Snipe—Migration of Quails—Snipe-Shooting—Persimmon Bushes.

THE entire neighbourhood is in an intense state of excitement, for the prospector for oil has disappeared. Since his arrest and release he had been living on the fat of the land, and had become a welcome guest at the houses of all the best families. A coal-oil company had also been formed. The shares were one hundred dollars each, with a capital of twenty thousand. So popular had he become that, a month after its organization, neither for love nor money could its scrip be obtained.

On the Embaras river, where there is a cavern that produces all kinds of unearthly sounds, and which emits such sulphurous smells as suggest that it is not far from the regions of his Satanic majesty, a shaft had been sunk. When it had reached the depth of three hundred feet, all the stockholders became sanguine, but with each additional hundred feet of descent, the value of the scrip decreased. So when the depth of nine hundred feet was reported, there was scarcely an investor, if the truth were known, who would not gladly have sold out at a loss of seventy-five per cent on the outlay. However, little of the scrip had changed hands, some sanguine people asserting that money would not purchase their shares; for as the " prospector" possessed five thousand dollars worth of stock, the reward for his discovery and services, and he still stuck to it, they were convinced that oil would be found sooner or later.

Thus matters stood when the whole vicinity was put in a violent state of commotion by the intelligence that oil had at last been struck. Those that had retained their stock congratulated themselves on their discretion, the unfortunates who had parted with theirs looked *triste*, refused to be comforted, and condemned their luck. This event had made poor men rich in imagination, and already one hundred dollars invested was regarded as having become five times, aye ten times that amount. What a crowd assembled that day when the long looked-for news was circulated on the banks of the Embaras.

The spot, at any previous time, never had presented the same attractions for mankind. Eating and drinking went on from morning to night beside the shaft; and I doubt not that some slept within sound of the laborious loud-sounding steam-engine. The report of oil coming from the shaft was no bogus story. The water that was raised from the bowels of the earth was coated with it, and the vicinity was already impregnated with its noxious fumes, so that Marie Farina's extract, or Jockey Club, or Lavender water never had so many ardent admirers. Many pronounced the odour of the oil fragrant; some I doubt not could have been found who even thought it equal to bourbon or old rye whiskey.

For days, affairs went on thus prosperously. The discoverer was lauded to the skies, and even the engineman and stoker came in for no small modicum of praise. All were good fellows, jolly good fellows, clever fellows; in fact, without compeers. How flattering this must have been to the promoter of the scheme; but, alas, he was absent at the time. Indisposition of a serious nature had called him East for medical advice, and he was reported to be so very ill that he could not communicate by telegraph or letter with any of his Company. After some weeks the oil became less abundant, the produce diminishing hourly, and ultimately it ceased altogether. This was very mysterious; all kinds of rumours were circulated as to the cause of a phenomenon so strange, but however impatient the stockholders became, they suppressed their feelings in the belief that all would be right as soon as the head of the enterprise returned to superintend operations; but he did not appear, and worse still, all trace of him had been lost. Still, when things grow wrong, people will not see them in their proper light, but in that of their own hopes and desires, and drowning men will cling to a straw.

At length the secret leaked out. A large quantity of petroleum had been brought to the well in a new boiler that was intended to take the place of that which had originally officiated, but was now worn out. Its contents were pumped into the shaft, or spilt about the neighbourhood; and the little game was so successfully played that these smart Western men were sold, and, to add to their feeling of humiliation, by a Secessionist, for it ultimately came to light that, after he had disposed of his stock at an immense premium in a Western city, he had directed his course for Dixie.

The stoker and engine-man, who were strangers, lost their enviable popularity so suddenly that they too thought fit to make themselves scarce. Well it was that they did so while yet able, for the infuriated investors would doubtless have vented such vengeance upon them as would have abruptly terminated their power ever afterwards to coal up or shut off steam.

At this period a large portion of the agricultural population was disaffected. Report even went so far as to say that of a moonlight night large bodies of men had been seen drilling on a neighbouring prairie; and it was ultimately discovered that the prospector for coal-oil was beyond doubt no other than a Confederate officer who had been dispatched to the North, to act as adjutant to those who had resolved to join the South in her struggle for independence.

Spring is making rapid advances, and if the weather continues open many days longer, snipe will make their appearance. On my ride home from the Embaras, for the first time since my residence here, I heard the ruffed grouse calling; a proof that they are soon going to mate. On the high ground at the back of the homestead exists a solitary family of these beautiful birds. Although opportunities have several times occurred when I might have possibly got a double shot at them, so far I have obstinately refused to kill the strangers. If they had been more abundant this would not have been the case, as before this date I have frequently, in Maine and more northern latitudes, made large bags of them.

Prairie chickens and American partridge are constantly to be seen exposed for sale, during the Winter months, in London and Liverpool markets; and therefore all possessed of means, or curious in Natural History, know them well by sight. But as the ruffed grouse is a comparative stranger to my countrymen, I deem it worthy of more than an ordinarily lengthened description.

This most noble specimen of game-bird has caused more disputes and mistakes in ornithology than probably all of its *confrères* put together. In the first place, it is universally misnamed, being incorrectly called "pheasant" in the Western and middle districts, while in Connecticut and Eastern New York it is equally wrongfully dubbed "partridge." Not only has it to suffer these misnomers, but it has frequently been confounded with a distinct species of the same genus, "the pinnated grouse" *(tetrao cupido)*, to which it has but little resemblance. Like our partridge, wild turkeys, &c., this species annually moves its quarters, always to return to its old haunts after

a short sojourn in some other locality; and,
consequently, many writers have asserted that
they are migratory, but there is as little, even
less ground for this statement, than there is for
the same erroneous impression in reference to the
two afore-mentioned game-birds.

According to my own observation, confirmed
by the opinion of those in whose veracity credence
can be placed, these temporary flittings can only
be accounted for by the lack of food which
happens with the change of the seasons; and so
cautious are they in their progress that this
erratic habit would scarcely be known, but that
they are frequently compelled to cross large
rivers to procure their necessary sustenance. In
the month of October these birds may annually
be seen in numerous detached parties on the
banks of the Ohio and Susquehanna, and their
numerous tributaries, waiting for a favourable
opportunity to cross to the southern shores. As
they are remarkably strong on the wing and
capable of long flights, they easily accomplish
their transit, when they scatter inland to return
in a few weeks. Frequently in that month they

will nearly entirely disappear from Northern Pennsylvania and Ohio, for the space of a few weeks, but ere grim Winter has placed his ice-bound foot upon the locality, their numbers will again have become as great as they were before their temporary disappearance. During the time of their peregrinations they are in a splendid condition, and afford excellent sport for the gunner, sometimes lying close before the dog, and even if flushed, satisfying themselves with the first limb of a tree that chance may throw in their way for a resting place, when frequently they are so heedless of danger as to permit the pot-hunter to knock over several from their perch ere the remainder will think of taking flight. Next to the wild turkey of Central and South Illinois and Indiana, we have no fowl which is reckoned a greater delicacy for the table, an opinion I endorse. Some *bon-vivants* may differ from me in this assertion, but I am convinced it can only result from their taste having become palled upon by too frequent enjoyment of what most deservedly is entitled to the appellation of *excellent.*

Wherever the surface of the country is hilly, irregular, and rocky, these birds are certain to abound (if it be neither too far north nor south), say from the latitude of Virginia to the most northern portions of Maine; the rough edges of streams, where the vegetation is dense, particularly if interspersed with evergreens, being their favourite retreats. However, I do not mean to assert that they will not be found in more level and accessible ground, for their nests will sometimes be seen, where least expected, throughout the region designated. In Northern Illinois, where the country is flat, the extraordinary "drumming" which the male makes I have frequently heard in the still calm of the Spring morning and evening, indicative to the sportsman of future coveys out of which he may some day expect to swell his bloodstained game-bag. In flight, unless the cover is dense, no birds afford a fairer mark, for their progress is generally straight, and is caused by numerous rapid flappings of the wings till sufficient impetus is obtained, when they sail much in the same manner as the prairie fowl. Nevertheless their flight is swift, and the noise which is made in flushing will often disconcert the tyro, causing him to shoot too quick, more birds of all species being missed by this impatience than by waiting too long. If a pupil will only display coolness, however bad his execution may be, he may still hope to become ultimately a good shot.

I fear that very many shoot for the sake of the bag, not from the proper spirit that should always predominate in the breast of the true sportsman and lover of nature; but if such should be the reader's case, let him cast aside his love of mere spoil, and on the first opportunity, if such a chance should ever occur, watch the habits and movements of this truly national bird. Having perceived his game upon the ground, feeding, which will frequently happen, let him secrete himself behind the nearest available log, and watch without bloodthirsty intent their graceful movements. No señorita of Andalusia could display more bewitching attractions. Their step is firm, carriage erect, and every movement grace. Many a time, from well-concealed places, have I gazed in admiration on the

handsomely feathered group, and slunk away
afterwards, with the guilty step of the midnight
assassin, my conscience accusing me of having
visited their retreat with murderous intent.
Gentle reader, there is as much pleasure in such
conduct as in having done a deed of charity.
Don't think me squeamish, my gun has done as
good work as most others, still I can desist from
slaughter, and glory in not having visited with
wanton destruction the unsuspecting brood.

In like manner the true sportsman does not
consider his dog a tool, but a companion and
assistant in the enjoyable sports of the field.
But man generally, I fear, is as much a tyrant as
the unreasoning portion of creation, as may so frequently be seen and proved by the brutal treatment his faithful setter or pointer will receive
when inadvertently he flushes game going down
wind; the ignoramus who hunts in a direction
which prevents the dog from using that organ
which is his only guide being really most to
blame. The gentlemanly manner of pursuing
the shooting of ruffed grouse is to use the setter,
but it is beyond a doubt that a smart cur dog,

who will bark at the birds and cause them to tree, will be more instrumental in obtaining a large bag. But consider the difference. With the first you cut down your game on the wing, the only honourable way of obtaining them, while with the second a sitting object is shot at, reflecting as little credit on the gunner (not sportsman) as slaughtering poultry in a farm-yard.

However, the pursuit of this sport is precarious, for whenever the birds have a chance they will betake themselves to the densest cover, where nothing but snap-shooting will avail, and once flushed, if by the gunner, it will be found almost impossible to mark them down. Even the young, before full grown, will rise with a whiz, alarming enough, for the most distant flight, when they will immediately drop and again hide themselves, frequently repeating the operation, and affording the sportsman no other indication of their manœuvre than the noise their tell-tale wings have made. Sometimes, when these birds are found on the side of a steep ravine or hill, as soon as they take wing, they dive for the foot of the declivity, then alter their course to the

right or left, and go in a direction so totally
different from the one expected, that it is more
than probable they cannot afterwards be discovered. However, in some portions of the
country, where the population is sparse and the
game less disturbed by human beings, they are
not so wily. While residing in Northern Maine,
especially far from cultivation, I found them so
tame and fearless of danger, that frequent
shots could be obtained before the covey was lost.
In Spring and Autumn it is possible to call them
up by beating an inflated bladder with a stick,
which makes a noise much resembling their own
drumming. In fact, I have succeeded in calling
almost every variety of American game, save
the prairie chicken or pinnated grouse. A further
peculiarity I would mention, which, though wondrous strange, is still true. When the snow is
soft and sufficiently deep, the birds will dive into
it, going several yards each time, and repeating
the manœuvre till they have either attained the
desirable distance to take flight, or have avoided
the observation of the intruder! In Winter, many
are taken in traps, how I will not describe, as I

would rather prevent such a custom than afford information to those capable of illegitimately destroying any of our valuable, handsome, indigenous species.

The ruffed grouse commence pairing early in April, when their presence may be known by the drumming which they make at dawn and sunset. As the season advances, this noise or call becomes so frequent that at all hours the curious sound can be heard. The manner of performing this drumming, many are ignorant of, so that it may not be inappropriate to explain it. The cock bird perches upon a log, erects his feathers, droops his tail and wings, throws his head back after the fashion of a gobbler, and struts about for a few moments, then stretches his neck forward and beats the air with his wings so rapidly as almost to produce a sound and reverberation like that of distant thunder. When the females hear this call, they fly to their lords, sail round them, and after alighting squat, as if tendering homage and submission to their august presence. Early in May the female lays from seven to twelve eggs in a primitive nest, composed of dried leaves and grasses, under the shelter of a log or old stump. The eggs are of a dull creamy colour, and about the size of those of the common bantam. As soon as hatched the young leave the nest and follow their mother, and in eight or ten days are able to use their wings a little. At this period, and even before the offspring leave the shell, the mother is most solicitous of her charge, and will successfully combat with either crow or hawk, striking the marauders with her wings, in the same way as the domestic fowl. But if the intruder be too formidable, then, after the manner of partridge, wild-duck, &c., she will droop her wings, feign lameness, and use every possible artifice to draw off attention from her helpless brood. While the female is engaged in family cares, the males congregate together, remaining so until late in Autumn, like other gay Lotharios, permitting all the onus of the charge of education to devolve upon their devoted spouses.

Their principal food consists of seeds and beans, including the wild and fox grape, of which they are particularly fond; also the tender succulent buds of many descriptions of plants, more particularly those of the different evergreens.

In conclusion, I will endeavour to describe correctly our subject, so that the ignorant may know of what he is owner when chance or skill has possessed him of this true table delicacy.

Eighteen inches long by twenty-four inches across the wing; plumage compact and glossy; feathers of the head narrow and elongated into a tuft; a long space on the neck destitute of feathers, which is hid by a bunch of long straight hackles, which, when the fowl is excited, stand out; wings short, broad, and rounded; the tail long, ample and fan-like; bill horn-colour, darker towards the tip; iris hazel; feet yellowish grey; upper part of the head and back of the neck a rich orange brown; back rich brown, marked longitudinally with oblong white marks; upper part of the wings the same, and pin feathers iron grey, with the outer edges cinnamon colour, diagonally crossed with darker colouring in narrow lines; tail cinnamon colour, with a dark bar across the extremity, and fine dark pencil marks regularly interspersed from root to tip; a dirty whitish line from bill to eye,

and continuing to back of head; breast and
lower portion of a light chocolate; under wings
a tuft of light, fawn-coloured feathers; stomach
dusky brown.

Of course, the colouring in different portions
of the country slightly varies, and the females
are less brilliant, but the description above given
will be found tolerably accurate.

From all the information I can obtain, snipe
make their appearance in this neighbourhood
about the 8th of March. This year they arrived
on the night of the 10th, or morning of the 11th,
for the previous day I had been over all the most
suitable places for their retreat, and failed to
flush a single bird. Yet on the 11th, upon exactly
the same beat, I found this description of game
most abundant. Persons possessed of a knowledge of natural history know that night is the time
selected by the members of this family to make
their migrations. Thus it occurs that it is very
seldom that even the closest observers of nature
have been afforded a chance to see snipe upon
their journeys. The flights in the Spring
of the year are doubtless very long, as the

birds which are killed immediately after their arrival are invariably thin and weak. The wind which they come by is southerly; thus one would be led to suppose that the instinct of migration is produced by excessive heat, which causes game to travel in the opposite direction from whence the inconveniently high temperature appears to originate. However, in Autumn, the cause is reversed, for cold exercises the same influence as warmth did earlier in the season. Not only in America, but in other parts of the world, will these be found to be the reasons that the feathered families have for making their periodical journeys. As one instance, I may mention the arrival and departure of quails from the southern shores of Europe and the Islands of the Mediterranean, as these birds are so well known by every sportsman and traveller who visits those parts of the world.

On my first day's experience of snipe-shooting, on the occasion previously adverted to, the birds were chiefly confined to those low-lying grounds on the edges of the sloughs, where the surface was hummocky. Between these excrescences was a considerable amount of cover, hiding a wet, black, slimy mud, which I should judge admirably adapted for boring. It was evident, from the reluctance the game evinced against taking wing, and the shortness of their flights when on the wing, that the birds were suffering from the fatigue resulting from a long and arduous journey.

In the vicinity of a retreat where a waggon track forded one of the swails, and where the surface was particularly soft and sloshy, the snipe were in such abundance that within the space of a few acres an enormous bag could have been made; however, not finding the birds in good condition, I satisfied myself with half-a-dozen couple, and went to a favourite stand to watch for wild fowl. The evening was too calm and warm to suit my purpose well, for when such is the case duck are later in coming on their feeding grounds, and evince considerable shyness in approaching them. Nevertheless, I obtained several shots, and when I had to cease shooting, from the increase of darkness, the broadbills were arriving in innumerable quantities. I have often thought what wholesale slaughter could have been made here with a stauncheon gun, used from a punt, for I have seen the water so covered with wild fowl that it appeared impossible for one more duck to crowd itself into a position among its fellows.

Next day I again went in search of snipe. Fresh arrivals had doubtless taken place, for without any apparent diminution in their numbers, they were scattered over a much wider extent of range—particularly the damp, low-lying ground on which stunted persimmon bushes grew. These shrubs afford admirable cover for such game, and as their height seldom exceeds three feet, they do not in the least interfere with the shooting; in fact, the only objection that can be urged against them is that they add considerably to the difficulty in finding the wounded and killed.

CHAPTER II.

Woman's Rights—Specimen of American Rhetoric on the
Negative side of the Question—John Stuart Mill—Law of
Divorce in Indiana—Painful Case—An American Sarah
Gamp—Treatment of Canine Disease—Cause and Cure of
Mange—Kennel Management—*Perseverentia vincit omnia.*

IN the neighbouring town I have heard the
most amusing and bitter denunciation of women's
rights. The speaker is a well known stump
orator who has worked himself into notoriety
through his force of delivery and bitterness of
language. In this neighbourhood women's rights
have been strongly and numerously advocated,
and so popular has the extension to females of
equal political privileges with the sterner sex
become, that it really required a very brave man
to rise up among a large audience of men and
women, all antagonistic in feelings to the speaker.

But the harangue was· equal to the occasion. Hisses and groans were alike disregarded, and by sheer determination alone he forced his audience to listen to him. He neither treated the subject gently, nor was any fear to express his mind for a moment evinced, till so great was the indignation of the listeners that the whole affair threatened to terminate in a free fight. If such had taken place, the orator must have got severely handled, as I heard several of the gentler sex express a determination to comb his wig, or scratch his eyes out, before they were done with him. I append a specimen of the Rhetoric.

"Few will dispute the fact that a bad woman is worse than a bad man, and, if any have the inclination to do so, let them visit our prisons and police courts, or cast a careful glance at the rum-besotted caricatures of the sex which are often to be seen staggering through the public streets. There is a certain circle marked by society, and, so long as women keep within it, they are very careful of their characters; but once let them step outside of it, and they become more thoroughly reckless than men ever become. Moreover, in connection with this moral argument, the very pertinent question suggests itself:—Were the women who have wielded power and ruled the destinies of nations eminent for any superior excellence of moral character? Was the fiery Cleopatra, who would ruin her kingdom for an Antony, a desirable ruler, or any of the following noted females of history? Theodora, the courtesan of the Circus in Constantinople, afterwards Empress of Rome; Catharine, of Russia, a prostitute; Elizabeth Petrovna, a woman indifferent to everything else except the indulgence of her passions; Catharine II. of Russia, satirized by Carlyle as 'a kind of she Louis XIV,' who shrank from no crime, not even the murder of her husband, and who always had a paramour as an officer of state; Queen Mary of England, who earned for herself the title of 'bloody;' Elizabeth, 'Good Queen Bess,' a foolish coquette, who toyed with subject after subject, and encouraged the attentions of the profligate Earl of Leicester, after he had so conveniently disposed of his wife—Amy Robsart—and whose inordinate vanity and paroxysms of passion made her ridiculous; Catharine de' Medici, authoress of the massacre of St Bartholomew's Day; Madame Pompadour, the capricious mistress and ruler of Louis XV, whose splendid vices cost France about 36,000,000 livres; Isabella, consort of Ferdinand the Catholic, who helped to establish the Spanish Inquisition; Marie Antoinette who by her childish frivolity hastened a bloody revolution; Anne, of England, a virtuous and conscientious woman, but so weak in character that she was governed by a subject, the Duchess of Marlborough. Maria Theresa, Empress of Germany, a resolute, masculine character, thoroughly competent to govern, shines brilliantly when contrasted with her compeers, but this exception serves rather to illustrate the rule than anything else. Very likely many will object to this historical comparison, and say that it is unfair to compare the women of the present with any of those potentates of the past. Well, so be it, and let the deposed Isabella of Spain answer their objection, or, that good woman but weak queen, Victoria, who has neglected all state duties because of a morbid grief."

Here the uproar became so serious that it was impossible for the speaker to be further heard, while the rush that was made to the platform on which he stood, admonished him that he had better depart while he could do so uninterruptedly. Consequently he vanished through the opening in his rear, not that I believe fear had aught to do with his retirement.

The rattle of wheels outside informed me that the orator had prudently determined to place distance between himself and the excited blue stockings. What a favourite would John Stuart Mill be here! But I suppose he gets too much petted at home to be induced to come abroad to receive such attentions.

From my knowledge of human nature, and from the immense influence which ladies wield over their husbands in political matters, I should fear that this brave denouncer of woman's rights had for ever ruined himself in the estimation of the public, and by his denouncement of the fair sex put a stop to all his advancement in public life.

In the State of Indiana any person can obtain

a divorce, after six weeks' residence in it, provided, when the case is called for hearing, there is no respondent, or the charges on which it is sought are proved against the defendant. The result of this is that strangers come from far and near to have the matrimonial tie unfastened ; and the professional men who devote their time and talents to this line of their profession, invariably amass large fortunes. As might be expected, it not unfrequently occurs that great injustice is done to innocent persons, in consequence of the responsibility of the tie of the Church being viewed in so unimportant a light that it can be broken at any moment, and on the most frivolous pretext. Let me add, however, in justice to the inhabitants of this State, that they do not avail themselves of their privilege in equal proportion to the number of visitors who come from other States, and that in the majority of instances, where the inhabitants have had recourse to it, the parties have been representatives of the lowest classes. I believe, however, it is the intention of the State Legislation to pass such laws as will much curtail the facilities which have previously existed for the dissolution of the bonds of matrimony. In a new country, society is on such an unstable basis, and the precursors of civilization are so frequently persons of the lowest standing, that abuses are certain to occur, but they are sure to be eradicated as soon as the proper-thinking and educated classes gain the ascendency.

American women have long been accredited with more than the usual capability of defending their rights; and there are ample grounds for believing that the character which has been attributed to them in this respect is correct, as cases frequently occur to prove. It is not always, however, by their own hands that their wrongs are avenged, but by those of relations or friends. A painful instance is here appended from the *St. Louis Times.*

" Samuel Van Norden has for nearly a year occupied apartments with his family in the third story of a brick block on Cass Avenue, and until very recently nothing has been observed by the neighbours which would indicate a lack of harmony or general satisfaction in the domestic relations. Van Norden has been married before, and in speaking of his former wife frequently mentioned the cause of her decease. By this first wife he has two children living, one of whom, a boy of thirteen years, has been a member of the present family. In some way, however, the suspicions of the last wife were aroused, and a few days ago, when she was informed by the little boy that his father had written to New York, she gave orders to the letter-carrier to have all letters left at the house instead of the shop. By this means she intercepted a letter written by Van Norden's New York wife to their joint husband. Concealing her information, she visited an attorney, whose name we could not learn, and placed the matter in his hands. On Thursday evening her husband called for her at the house of a friend, and they walked home quietly together, as if nothing had happened. As soon, however, as they entered their rooms, he turned upon her and demanded the letter, of which, it seems, he had obtained some knowledge. She refused to comply with his request, or tell him anything, whereupon he knocked her down,

with her babe in her arms, and otherwise mal-
treated her. Then, taking his razor, he proceeded
to cut into shreds valuable dresses and clothing
which she had purchased with money that belonged to her before her marriage. The neighbours were aroused by her screams, and a large
crowd collected in the vicinity. An officer ap-
pearing shortly after, the man was arrested
and taken to the Third District station on a
charge of disturbing the peace. The case was
brought up in court, and continued for several
days.

"Van Norden, upon gaining his liberty, went
back to the house and found the rooms unoc-
cupied, his wife having gone to a neighbour's for
fear of further injury. He at once began to take
up the carpets and put the furniture in a condition to be taken away, and while thus engaged
alone in the rooms, the father of the misused wife
was seen to enter the house. From the injured
man's statement it seems that the father, whose
name is John Irvine, and who lives in East St.
Louis, entered the room where Van Norden was
at work, and said:—'Here you are, then,' or

something similar, and without another word raised his pistol and fired two shots, both of which took effect. Van Norden cried: 'Don't, for God's sake,' and rushed to the door to escape. He first ran out into the passage and then turned and started down stairs. This brought him face to face with the old man, who had started after him. Irvine then fired a third shot, the ball grazing Van Norden. The wounded man ran down both flights of stairs out into the street, and nearly a block up Cass Avenue, finally taking refuge in a blacksmith's shop near Sixteenth Street.

"Irvine followed him down stairs out on the street, and then down an alley, and ran across some vacant lots to the Mullanphy Home, thence making his way rapidly to the river, and crossing at the Venice ferry. Van Norden immediately sat down on a trestle, after entering the shop, and was soon taken with fainting fits and vomiting of blood. Dr. Eaton was called, and upon a hasty examination it was found that one ball had penetrated the chest, and apparently lodged in the lungs. The other ball had entered the abdomen a little to the right of the centre and passed through the body, coming out, probably, just below the kidneys. A carriage was at once secured, and the sufferer taken to the hospital. Upon examination there, the surgeons gave it as their opinion that the man cannot possibly recover, and that his death might be expected at any moment.

"Not long after the time when Mrs. Van Norden, as she supposed herself to be, visited the attorney with the intercepted letter, a search was instituted among the records of East St. Louis to see whether her marriage was recorded. No trace of such a record could be found, and it was discovered that the ceremony had been performed by some vagabond shyster without any authority whatever. As soon as the news of this double disgrace came to the father of the wronged woman, he became very much excited and started for St. Louis. While on his way to the house he called on some friends, talked about his troubles, and said he was going up to see about it. Strong efforts were made to dissuade him from his purpose, which had the apparent effect of calming him down, but he soon slipped out unnoticed and made his way to the scene of the tragedy. Yesterday afternoon officers were despatched to East St. Louis in search of him, when it was found that he lived just east of the first toll-gate on the Collinsville road. He had been there and told his wife the particulars of the occurrence, and said he was going away to stay until he learned how the wounds resulted, but affirmed that he would ultimately give himself up to the authorities. He is a man of about six feet in height, with dark hair and thin brown chin whiskers. He was still at large up to a late hour last night. The sham ceremony was performed six years ago, and all this time the parties have been living together amicably, although the husband's character has not been above reproach. Van Norden was a boss-carpenter and stair-builder, and had some property in the upper part of the city. The family lived in good style, and were generally looked up to as exceptionally free from domestic differences."

There is a superior description of Sarah Gamp

in this neighbourhood—only she is an American instead of an English specimen of that world-wide known character. She is a woman of great energy and force of character, glories in the non-possession of any feminine weaknesses, always dresses in a costume that represents the fashions of a mediæval age, and is the fear and aversion of all the male population that have seen thirty summers, and are not yet entered into the bonds of matrimony. She has also the reputation of being almost ubiquitous, turning up at all places and times when least expected; and whether the assembly that she, thus un-invited, thrusts herself upon be rich or poor, illiterate or educated, she, by virtue of a right, the origin which no one can tell, assumes to herself the direction of all its proceedings. If a charity be started, it matters not whether it be to obtain warming-pans for the niggers or re-frigerators for the Esquimaux, she is certain to become principal beggar, more especially in those cases in which the quiet eloquence of curates fails to induce the rich to open their purse-strings. There are few, however, that would not sooner respond to the clergyman's calls for charity than suffer themselves to be interviewed and bullied by this strong-minded specimen of the weaker sex.

My landlord is a good fellow, but has a tendency to keep the strings of his purse, which holds his dollars and cents, very tightly drawn. He thoroughly believes that charity begins at home, and that most persons owe the low state of their finances either to indolence or idleness. The curate had called one morning at our residence, and had failed to extract a subscription for some unfortunate refugees from the south who had found their way into the town in a fearful state of penury. In addition to his dislike to parting with money, there was another reason which kept his purse closed. My landlord, although he had the sense to keep it to himself, was a thorough Southern sympathiser, and believed that every man born south of Mason and Dixon's line, who deserted his country in the day of her tribulation, deserved any fate, no matter how severe. The curate had been gone some hours, and my friend was chuckling over his success

in having successfully escaped the ungenial
obligation of putting his hand into his pocket,
when a very masculine rap was heard at the
door of our sitting-room. It was after dinner,
and the decanters were on the table, while we
were pleasantly smoking our pipes.

The hour was so late that no one could be
expected to disturb our ease, except some of the
farm-servants to obtain instructions for the
guidance of the next day's labour. With a
stentorian voice, therefore, he called out, " Come
in," and to his disgust and mine, there entered the
terror of all the single men in the vicinity. Any
other lady would have sent her name up before
coming so far on the premises, but this worthy
woman was too well acquainted with finesse to
pursue such a course—fearing she might have
been told that no one was at home, or that the
object of her visit was engaged on pressing private
affairs which rendered him unable to grant any
one an interview. My landlord, however, was
cornered, and he knew it, but was resolved not
to strike his flag until compelled.

The object of the lady's visit was not stated

until she had been requested to take something both hot and strong, which was declined. When she did apply herself to her task, her tongue wagged most fluently. "There was no accounting," she said, "for the utter want of charity some persons possessed, although they professed to be members of the Church. Was it not a disgrace that a stranger (meaning me) should subscribe to a home charity, when a citizen of the great Republic would not do so. Such conduct, however, was only what she expected from a man of his years (forty-five), who had never been able to sink his selfish feelings, and take unto himself a wife."

My friend attempted to respond, but it was no use, for not a word could he get in edge-ways or otherwise. At length, losing all patience, he exclaimed,

"Madam, if you have a brother send him to me, and I will be able to settle this difficulty."

The lady responded. "If I had a brother, Sir, do you suppose I would trust this sacred duty in the hands of one of your sex? No, Sir, I

would not; for he, as well as you, would doubtless be incapable of performing those duties
which require mind and decision of character."
For more than an hour she held forth, one
moment arguing and at another upbraiding, till,
in his ardent desire to terminate the interview,
my companion paid up under protest. As our
visitor left the room, which she did upon my
requesting her to have a glass of something
strong, she wound up by saying, "She was not
done with my host yet, for she should feel it
her duty to look out for a partner for him, not
one of your snips of girls which old fools were
always running after; but one of more mature
years, who would imbue him with some of the
milk of human kindness, and teach him his duty
towards his fellow-men."

The river, having again subsided into its
proper channel, has ceased to be "booming," as
the people here call it when out of its banks.
The débris and wash which it has left behind
gives the landscape a most wintry look, but
this desolate appearance will not long remain,
for this refuse acts as a most powerful manure,

and causes the vegetation, in the course of Spring, to burst forth much earlier than it otherwise would. Mosquitoes, however, have made their appearance, their presence being accounted for by the late overflow. They are not in sufficient numbers however to be very troublesome.

I am convinced that my favourite bitch has caught mange. Hitherto my dogs have been so very free from all such ailments, that I feel certain it is to be attributed to contagion, more especially as I always pay extreme attention to cleanliness in my kennel.

The majority of works that treat upon the dog assert that this repulsive disease has several species or varieties; for myself, I do not pretend to be sufficiently skilled to pronounce an opinion, and therefore will only write of the two different kinds that have come under my own notice. It is not my intention, however to write a long and scientific essay on this subject, but simply to give my brother sportsmen the benefit of my lengthened experience. I believe that, without great scientific attainments, any person,

with due care and attention, can keep a
kennel healthy, unless he should have the
misfortune to get diseased stock among his favourites.

Mange is undoubtedly contracted by bad feeding, neglect, filth, or want of cleanliness, unless
in cases of contagion, and so thoroughly am I
convinced of this that, were I to visit a kennel,
whomsoever it might belong to, and find that his
animals were afflicted with this disgusting disease,
I should at once pronounce him to be no sportsman, in the proper acceptation of the word,
always provided it had not been engendered as
I believe in the present case. A very worthy
friend and devoted admirer of field-sports used
to say that he would refuse an introduction to
any man, even if he were a prime minister, if
he kept a mangy kennel. This complaint is
almost universal, there being scarcely a hamlet
or village that has not one or more homeless,
masterless, neglected, half-starved curs which
come across us daily, an eye-sore to all humane
beholders, and a burden to themselves, whom it
would be charitable to knock on the head.

All authorities are decided that this ailment is caused by the lodgement of minute animalculæ under the skin, the incessant burrowing of which causes intense irritation. In the majority of cases it is produced by contact, although occasionally it is hereditary. Sometimes, for instance, a mangy slut will bear pups similarly affected; and in such cases as these it is much more difficult to cure than in the former.

The varieties of the complaint with which I am acquainted are the scabby and the red. The former, which is much the more common, is less violent in its nature, and easier cured. The distinguishing features between the two are that in the red mange the skin appears smooth and polished, of an angry colour, with nearly entire loss of hair, while the scabby is white and scurvy with small sores and a frequent watery discharge from the pores of the skin. In handling animals thus afflicted, you should be careful to wash your hands immediately afterwards, as there have been numerous instances of human beings contracting this complaint. Particular care should also be taken to prevent dogs so afflicted from entering a stable, as, from its highly contagious nature, horses are very susceptible of its influence, and, when it has gained headway, it is very troublesome to cure them of it, rendering the animal very unsightly for a lengthened period, from the loss of his hair in blotches all over the affected parts of the carcase. Nevertheless, there are few stages in which, with judicious and careful treatment, your labours to effect a cure will not be rewarded with success. The desired end may be slowly attained, but persevere, and, in nine instances out of ten, you will be victorious.

My old friend Captain Peel, 1st Royal Regiment, so well known as the author of one of the most practical works on kennel management, had a perfect mania for securing all kinds of disease-stricken canines on which to operate; and on one occasion, while residing with him at Gibraltar, he captured a pointer slut so completely covered with mange that she was disgusting to look at. Much to the horror of his neighbours, who all kept horses and dogs, he had her tied up in an outhouse in the vicinity. There was much chuckling at what to all appeared an insane attempt to doctor a case so far gone. Morning and evening he regularly attended to superintend and see his orders carried out, and success was his reward; for, in two months after, he had a healthy dog, which proved itself most valuable at a future date in the field—*perseverentia vincit omnia*. I have seldom had the misfortune to have any of my pets afflicted with this disorder, but have frequently seen it treated. I have also, on many occasions, advised friends, who supposed that I had more skill and knowledge than they possessed themselves, and in every instance success followed my efforts. I will here append the recipes I use.

Red Mange.—Rub your dog well with mercurial ointment, but great care must be taken to prevent his getting cold, as in that case you will probably lose him. On the first appearance of the disease, smearing only the affected parts will suffice. Powdered aloes should be mixed with the ointment, to prevent the animal licking himself.

Scabby Mange.—Mix brimstone finely powdered with hogs' lard, in equal proportions; rub your patient with this unguent daily for from six to ten days, at the same time administering some opening medicine. Another cure which I have found excellent is :—sulphur, two ounces; aloes, two drachms; mercurial ointment, two drachms; hogs' lard, four ounces. Let all be mixed well together, and rub the patient with it once daily for a week.

In making use of either of the above recipes in which mercury is used—although aloes have been added to prevent the dog licking himself—it would be as well to place a stiff leather stock upon his neck, sufficiently long to reach from the shoulders to the ears.

CHAPTER III.

An Ex-Pugilist—A Pretty Daughter and her Suitors—A Military Hero—Single-Stick—A Challenge accepted for me without my Knowledge—Conditions of the Contest—A Hit, a very Palpable Hit—A Fight—Commencement of the Fishing Season—Fish caught in the Wabash and its Tributaries—Sensation Articles.

IN a neighbouring town lives an Englishman, proprietor of a public-house, whom I have previously mentioned. In early youth, before coming across the Atlantic, he had figured as a pugilist and dog-fancier, and, although now well advanced in years, is so handy with his maulies, that it would take more than an average amateur to give him a drubbing. Of course he is fond of the art in which he excels, and in his cups holds forth to an attentive crowd on the deeds of prowess he has performed in days gone by. He has taken a wonderful fancy to me, and when I visit him there is nothing in his house that is not at my service. In fact, so determined is his hospitality, that I had ultimately to inform him that I would cease to be his visitor, unless he permitted me to pay my score. With such a host, is it to be wondered at that all who love field-sports, or excel in the practice of them, make his hostelry a house of call? If the champion of the P. R. himself were passing this way, he doubtless would find time to pay a visit to this not at all unworthy representative of the British nation, for I must state that he is held in equally favourable repute by parson, magistrate, tradesman, and tramp.

He has also a blushing buxom lass for a daughter, whose age is not far off twenty summers, and the fame of whose beauty has been circulated far and wide. Many a swain who drops in to see the old man and taste his good cheer, has also an eye to his daughter, in whose good graces he tries to establish himself. The young lady, who has not yet made any selection, or shown any preference, has abundance of suitors, the number daily increasing, and with them the business of her father's establishment. Although I have no designs in this quarter, it would be folly not to confess that my horse's head was not oftener guided towards her father's inn than if she had been less attractive would have been the case.

Among the various suitors is a *ci-devant* corporal of one of our own regiments of Light Dragoons, now a major in the American Volunteer Service. He is a splendid representative of the swash-buckler type, and never loses an opportunity of descanting on the numerous deeds of prowess he has performed. That he is pluck personified there can be no doubt, for in his possession are documents from state authorities recognising in strong terms the value of his services. Still he is a tremendous boaster, and blows his own horn with such energy that the nervous listen trembling to the narrative of his exploits. With all these advantages, however, he cannot carry by assault the heart of his countrywoman. All overtures heretofore have been successfully repulsed, and disappointment has

soured his temper and made him a nui-
sance.

One of his numerous ideas is that he is the
best swordsman that ever drew a sabre. If brute
strength were sufficient to make him so, then
he undoubtedly ought to excel all competitors.
The better to carry out his love affair he had
taken up his residence at the tavern ; but having
quarrelled with several of the ex-pugilist's best
patrons, and made himself obnoxious to them,
that worthy had determined to get rid of him at
any price. One evening the major in his cups
was enlarging upon his scientific attainments in
the use of single-stick, and when declaring he
could beat the whole world, the host stopped
him with the inquiry if for a matter of a few
dollars he would like a bout with a friend of his
who sometimes paid him a visit. Money being
evidently abundant with both, a hundred dollars
a side was soon deposited in the safe keeping of
a trustworthy stakeholder.

Now who do you think had been selected by Old
Boniface to do battle for his dollars ? I, no
other than I ! and that without asking the simple

and proper question, whether I was willing. There was an indifference to my feelings in the affair, and a confidence in my ability to serve him that were truly delightful. The result, it is true, might be to him the loss of a few dollars. That was nothing. On me it might entail a broken head or a few bruises. That was even less. Single-sticks were accordingly got ready, and the forthcoming contest was eagerly discussed by the chosen few to whom the secret was confided. Not a whisper, however, in reference to the matter had floated to my ear, and I was perfectly unconscious of the *mêlée* in which I was bound to figure so prominently the day after the bets were made.

Tired and thirsty from a long and unsuccessful deer-hunt, I one day galloped up to the hotel or tavern, with the hopes of there refreshing the inward-man. The sharp notes from my pony's hoofs called out the daughter and groom. To the latter I handed my trusty steed, while to the former I proffered a kiss as soon as we were sufficiently past the entrance of the house to be out of the sight of witnesses. Rose, for such was her name, was a jolly girl to kiss, possessing full pouting lips of the colour of the flower after which she was named. I fear I lingered too long in the enjoyment of the luxury, for when I turned round I found myself in the presence of the fire-eater, whose look plainly expressed a wish to give me such a brace of shakes as he alone could give.

If I had been caught by the governor, as Rose's father was generally denominated, I most certainly should have felt abashed, but the interruption of this unknown animal rather irritated me. So I released the laughing girl's waist, and looked as I felt, the insulted man. Although we confronted each other for several seconds, not a word was spoken on either side. At length whistling, "The Laird of Cock-pen," I brushed past the fellow and entered the *salle-à-manger*.

Mine host welcomed me with more than his usual warmth, and while we were discussing the various incidents connected with my unsuccessful hunt, the ex-corporal of Dragoons entered the room, took a seat, and at every opportunity eyed me with optics the light of which resembled that of the green-eyed monster. Friend after friend dropped in, and although every subject of conversation was brought on the *tapis*, not one broached the anticipated bout of single-stick, and thus I chaffed and laughed, innocent of any knowledge of the storm that was brewing. At length Boniface called over the antagonist whom my friends desired to pit me against, and making some trifling apology, introduced us to each other, for previously I had never met him. We bowed, and it was evident there was no love lost between us. Our host, addressing himself to my opponent, said,

"This is the gentleman that you have heard me mention as a proficient in single-stick." To this the major raised his cap, and expressed himself highly gratified in making the acquaintance of one who was conversant with so noble a science, adding, almost in the words of Colonel Damas, "that such being the case it was a guarantee of my gentility.". Bowing in return for so handsome a compliment, I retired to enjoy my lunch, of which I was in wondrous need.

At length, when my meal was almost finished, the landlord joined me, and in a careless way informed me that he and several of my friends wished me to cross sticks with the gentleman to whom he had just introduced me. I urged, as an excuse, that sticks could not be obtained. " They are already provided," he said. I was urged so much that, after exhausting every excuse I could think of, I positively refused to act any part in the matter, and for a time it appeared to drop. The Major drank frequently and deeply, and his voice, while talking with his friends, became so violent that it was apparent he was not in the best of humours.

When preparing to take my departure, he crossed the room and addressed himself to me. " Surely," he said, " you are not afraid to gratify so many in their desire to see us fence. Possibly you do not consider me your equal in standing, and will not so far honour me as to meet me in a friendly bout, or were you only joking in the matter, and actually knew nothing of the subject you professed a knowledge of?" When commencing his remarks he was cool and collected, but as he proceeded he became more excited, till at the end no one could avoid seeing that he was displeased. None of the spectators could see sufficient grounds for my objection, and therefore thought that I was undeserving of sympathy.

When in the army, I was so proficient in single-stickfencing that I constantly practised it, and so far excelled in the exercise that it was seldom I got beaten. My success had made me partial to the sport, but that was several years ago, and now I feared I might be very rusty and have lost all that flexibility of the wrist so necessary to an expert. I could not stand this badgering, however, and from want of decision actually consented to act in opposition to my true feelings and better judgment. My determination was hailed with applause, and I at once rose fifty per cent in the estimation of all present.

The preliminaries were arranged. The host was to be umpire, and a covered skittle-alley the battle-field. The stick that was handed me was a splendid piece of rock elm, as tough as a withe and as light as a feather—just such as the most fastidious would select to make nice play with.

Before commencing work, it was decided that, whenever either got touched, he was to drop his stick as an acknowledgment, and that whoever received the first three cuts was to be deemed the loser. If either lost his temper, the contest was to cease, and the offender to be declared vanquished.

It was evident that the Major, who had drunk too much, did not appear under advantageous circumstances, as the issue proved. To feel my foe I placed myself on the defensive, while he adopted the very policy that was calculated to do him injury. In a few moments I knew the calibre of my man, and it was far from being so high as I had anticipated. So a chance occurring, I struck from beneath upwards, and touched his elbow. It certainly was a very light touch, but sufficient. He refused, however, to acknowledge that my stick had got home. The disputed point was waived, and we commenced again. Next time I inwardly determined, in order to prevent any doubts, to employ sufficient force. Three or four successful guards were then executed by me, when I obtained a chance, and laid in a tolerable upper-cut over the lower portion of the sword-arm. Feeling himself overweighted, or burning with passion at the blow, his anger augmented with the fumes of the spirit he had drunk, and he rushed at me. The blows became fast and furious, and in quick succession every point had to be guarded. But I retained my presence of mind, and determined not to balk his fancy. He overreached himself in endeavouring to strike my leg, and I gave him a reminder down the back of the head and shoulders. In a fury he hurled his stick to the winds, and doubling his fists he made for me. I had no fancy for such a contest, but apparently could not avoid it. The ex-pugilist, however, came in between us. My late antagonist did not for an instant appear to regret the interference, but rushed at his foe like a fury. After a pass or two, he got one on the nob; in fact, the old man played with him for several minutes without receiving a scratch. The belligerents were

then separated by the spectators, and it is almost
needless to add that the Major the day after
left the neighbourhood, and not in company with
the bonny Rose.

The fishing season having now fairly commenced, I made my *début* with great success—
for I doubt much if any man could be found
strong enough to carry the produce of my day's
sport. Unfortunately, liver is the only bait that
can be employed here successfully, unless when
angling for black bass, and even then fish do not
appear to rise as readily to the fly in the Wabash
as they do in New Brunswick, Canada, and East-
tern New York.

The fish most frequently caught in the waters
and tributaries of the Wabash are buffalo fish,
black bass, rock bass, pike-perch, and yellow
perch. The first of these (buffalo fish) is a true
carp, and grows to an enormous size. Scarcely
any surprise is expressed when one of the weight
of thirty or even forty pounds is captured. Their
habits are very peculiar. They appear in and
disappear from waters in the most mysterious
manner. I have never heard any explanation of

the cause of these migrations, but should imagine they might be attributed to change of temperature and the approach of the breeding season. In early Spring, when the rivers overflow their banks from the breaking up of ice and the melting of snow, these fish appear in immense numbers, forcing their way forward, even when there is barely room to swim, with the advance waters of the threatening inundation. Talk of herrings in a cask, to express numbers, the *simile* is equally applicable when speaking of this western irruption of the inhabitants of the Wabash.

But the moment the tide turns and the flood commences to ebb, with one accord, like a terror-stricken army, they fly for the deeper waters of the parent stream. Sloughs and ponds are reached by these annual inundations of neighbouring rivers; and into these many straggling buffalo fish find their way. They can be seen in them every calm morning or evening, enjoying the luxury of the sun's rays when they have not the fierce glow of mid-day. As an article of human food they are excellent, and may be served up, cooked in almost endless ways, yet always palatable. Unfortunately, however, they are of little or no value to the sportsman, as it is extremely seldom that they can be captured with hook and line.

Many persons imagine that these carp, after the manner of salmon, annually pay a visit to the sea. From observation and inquiry I am inclined to believe such to be the case. They might be called, not improperly, the salmon of the Mississippi. Such a name, however, would never be popular among our countrymen, for we are in the habit of associating in our minds with the word salmon all that is game, bright, and beautiful in shape.

The next inhabitant of the Wabash I have named is the black bass. I will borrow a description of it from Mr. Roseveldt, an author who is no mean authority on such subjects. "This fish has innumerable scientific names, while it can scarcely be said to have any distinctive popular one. Bass, either alone or with some additional appellation, is applied by common usage to almost the entire perch family (in America), while scientific men are at as great a loss for appropriate nomenclature or accurate distinctions. There are probably several species classed under the same name as this fish, and it differs greatly in colour and appearance according to its food, water, or locality.

" There is no doubt that all fish, and more especially trout, change their hues according to the colour of the water they inhabit, or even to the light and shade of their favourite haunts. It is supposed they assimilate to the bottom where they are found, a provision of nature to protect them from their enemies in the air. Unquestionably those of the species seen in clear pellucid streams present a very different appearance from those found in muddy sluggish brooks. Black bass are said to possess the power of changing their colour at will, as they have been known to do so when confined in a vessel of water."

After the above quotation, the reader doubtless will agree with me that the fish I write of is worthy of much attention, more particularly when I add that it combines several qualities, namely, gameness when hooked, greediness of appetite, and beauty of form. It is at the same time highly esteemed as an article of food. I will quote further from the author previously alluded to.

"They will take minnows, shiners, grass-hoppers, frogs, worms, or almost anything else that can be called bait. They may be fished for with good stout tackle, gut leaders, a reel, and an ordinary bass (bait) rod, in the same manner as fish are generally captured by boys and blockheads." The writer is a great proficient in trout-fishing, and an advocate for the use of the lightest and most delicate tackle.

"In June they affect the grassy bottom, in water ten or fifteen feet deep, but as the season advances they resort to the rocky shoals and rapid currents, where they are taken on and after the middle of July by sportsmen with the fly."

Although the author had the black bass of the north under his observation when writing this, his remarks equally apply to the fish of the Wabash—the average weight of which is about three pounds, the very largest barely reaching five.

Independent of the natural bait which these fish take freely, a small trolling spoon, slightly sunk beneath the surface, has been often found a most killing lure, more so even than the artificial fly, which is frequently used with good effect.

The rock bass is an entirely different species from the black bass, although frequently confounded with it. It is a free feeder, and not without considerable gameness. Its weight seldom exceeds three-quarters of a pound. As an article of food it much resembles our English perch.

The pike-perch, which comes next, is a splendid fish to look at, and capital upon the table, but the most arrant cur that ever had the misfortune to be captured with a hook. These fish being peculiar to the rivers of this part of the Western Continent, much controversy has been provoked regarding their origin, many asserting that they are a hybrid produced by the interbreeding of pike and perch. What has given birth to this supposition I cannot tell, for there is not the slightest resemblance between this fish and the two varieties mentioned. The pike-perch is frequently called the Ohio salmon, and I have heard persons say that it was identical with the *salmo salar*; but this is an erroneous assertion, and could only be advanced by persons incapable of offering an opinion. In Winter they perfectly swarm underneath the rapids situated at Mount Carmel, when they take the bait freely. In Summer they entirely disappear, and are supposed to go to the sea. Their average weight is about ten pounds.

This species must not be confounded with a similar fish frequently taken below the falls at Louisville, which seldom exceeds a pound in weight.

The yellow perch, the last on the list, is a splendid fish to look at, and that is his only good quality. He is credited with the possession of a most voracious appetite. Sometimes the yellow perch are so numerous that it is impossible to take other fish, as they seize the bait the moment it touches the water. In size they vary much, according to situation, but it is no uncommon thing to find them turn the scale at fifteen pounds.

The laws against scandal do not appear to be enforced in America with the same vigour as in the United Kingdom, or it may be that the people in the former fear consequences less, and thus become more reckless. The consequence is that the public papers constantly print the most glaring mis-statements of circumstances, and do not hesitate to publish the most flagrant libels upon those to whom they are politically or personally opposed.

Events which should be kept secret, because from their nature they have a tendency to debauch the minds of young and inexperienced persons, are openly detailed in their newspapers. The authorities should consider it a duty to use all their power to suppress what are here called sensation articles; as they are calculated to sow seed in the minds of the innocent, certain to ripen in time and produce the most injurious fruit. I am reluctant to justify the adverse feelings with which I regard such prostitution of the press, because it would be inappropriate in me to select for reproduction an example of those articles for the publication of which I condemn others.

In proof, however, that my statement is not unfounded, I select with due consideration for the morals of the reading public, the following example, extracted from one of the Western periodicals :

"Those at all familiar with St. Charles Street are aware that in one of its public resorts a man meets a strange mixture of society. The mimic stage, the song and dance, unite to make the rosy hours go by with flying feet—and the charms of conviviality are not without their attractions. The first floor is devoted to the miniature theatre ; the second story is devoted to a bar, and what is popularly called 'a wine-room.' In this last-named place, usually, very select parties are assembled. Gentlemen with plethoric purses meet there the radiant nymphs of the stage—the stars regnant of the little theatre. A round table in the centre of the room is covered with glasses and decanters of wines; and those whose tastes incline them that way ' drink with the fair damsels who abide therein,' and are merry.

" Into this apartment, Wednesday night, was ushered a police Commissioner—a fat and jolly-looking fellow, as rosy as Bacchus himself, and known among his intimate friends as "Bobby." Evidently the atmosphere of the place was congenial to him, and for the nonce he laid aside the dignity of official station and became a thorough bacchanal. The generous wine inclined his heart to dalliance, and the smiles of the bewitching syrens almost made him believe that he had stumbled on Mohammed's paradise; so strange a fascination did these dark-eyed, golden-haired houris exert upon his tender police heart. Never in his life had he met with a scene so enchanting.

The wine flowed in brimming glasses, and with each libation the official toasted a radiant divinity. But ambrosial nectar, when taken in too great quantities, affected the standing of

Olympian Jupiter, and champagne was equally potent with our convivial official. His eyes began to assume a leerish sort of jollity that showed he was fast approaching that condition in which he would be found " fit for treason, stratagem, and spoil." His compliments grew more profuse as his utterance clogged, and at last the sturdy disciplinarian of the police became as soft a wooer as was the Trojan youth who beguiled the bride of Menelaus.

"One female, however, more than the rest, seemed to exercise a potent influence over the official. She was thin and angular, it is true, and her nose was red, but these peculiarities were fuel to the passion of the Commissioner. He saw her through a haze of champagne, and she looked to him as radiant as the Medicean Venus.

" 'Wilt thou kiss me ?' lisped the maudlin official.

" 'Sir!' indignantly aspirated the ballet dancer.

"And again the *champagne smile* stole invitingly across the Commissioner's face.

"'You do not know me,' he said; 'I can have this house arrested, and you thrown into a dungeon. I'm powerful—*me big Ingun!*' he exclaimed, waxing wroth.

"The proprietor of the establishment, hearing loud words and fearing a raid similar to those he had recently experienced before, hastened to appease his official visitor.

"'My dear sir,' he said, 'be calm; the girl shall kiss you. It is only modest that she is; pray, sir, pardon her. She fails to appreciate the honour that you do her.'

"'Well, that's all right; but she ought to know I can have her arrested.'

"'Oh, yes, sir, she now perfectly understands that fact.'

"'You say she's modest.'

"'Oh, yes, sir.'

"'Well, then, she can kiss me for my mother,' said the maudlin Adonis.

"And she did."

With such trash all the papers abound. I do not mean to say that in the above extract there is not a basis of truth to work upon, but the greater portion is evidently exaggeration.

CHAPTER IV.

A BUSY season has now commenced, ploughing and planting are the order of the day, and every available hand is employed. Maize or Indian corn being a staple here, and not cultivated at home, I shall endeavour to describe the process of their cultivation.

Late and early frosts being frequent in England, and the evenings in Summer being destitute of a heat almost tropical in its intensity, we do not succeed in cultivating Indian corn.

There is, however, no more useful grain to be found on the face of the globe, it being equally suited for food for man and beast. In the United States. it is a favourite crop, and in the southern portion of Illinois and Indiana I believe it is cultivated with greater success than elsewhere upon the great American continent.

In the neighbourhood where I am living, it is no uncommon thing to find the straw ten or twelve feet long, while the cob is not rarely fifteen inches from shoulder to point, and I have been informed that instances are not wanting where one hundred bushels of maize have been taken off an acre.

The cultivation of Indian corn is not difficult, and is conducted after the following manner. The soil is, in the first place, well ploughed, and then cross-ploughed, so as to divide it into hillocks about three feet apart, in each of which are deposited from three to five grains of maize. When the grain has grown to an altitude of a foot or more, the ground is again ploughed or hoed, in order to throw the soil better around the plants, as well as to keep down the weeds which, if the field is neglected, are certain to spring up in great profusion, and by absorbing a large portion of the nutriment of the ground, materially injure the coming crop of maize. In early days, if frost occurs, the tender plants are sure to suffer much damage; but when the warm days and nights of the American Summer set in they are safe, and the progress of their growth is something that in the inexperienced would create astonishment. If the Indian corn should have become ripe by the end of September, it is not, as a rule, gathered till the frosts of Autumn have set in, when the ears are plucked from the stems, which are left standing for the use of the stock when Winter has so far advanced as to destroy all other green food.

Horses, horned cattle, and hogs alike eat this succulent grain, and fatten on it. The wild animals derive a large portion of their support from it, the birds of the air are partial to it, and man eats it in its green state cooked in various ways, or, when it is ripe, ground into meal from which bread and porridge are made.

A more beautiful crop than maize is not to be found in any part of the world. In earliest Summer it is in colour the most verdant green, in Autumn the richest yellow, and when the breezes wander over its surface, while the rays of the bright sun play upon its feathery tops, it appears to change its shade with every movement. A s the various stems rustle together, they produce a soft musical sound like the strains that emanate from the water of a distant and rapid brook.

One variety of Indian corn, called ' brown corn,' does not produce a cob, but a feathery tassel covered with diminutive seeds. From this plant is manufactured the ordinary household broom used in the country ; and a capital sweeper it is, bearing favourable comparison with the implements of any country used for the same purpose.

A few days ago the police warned me that a ring which I was in the habit of wearing had attracted the cupidity of so many disreputable persons that they thought it better that I should cease to display it on my finger. As this ring was an old favourite, I hesitated to follow their advice, not that I cared for jewelry, quite the reverse. It had been my custom for some time back to come into town of an evening, about sunset, and return about midnight, but soon after receiving this information I rode my pony to the bridge, where I tied him, and left him till I required his services on my return.

That evening I was kept so much later than usual that, when I reached the spot where my mount had been left, it possibly had passed midnight, and to my surprise my nag was not to be seen. The night was dark and blustery. As there were no reasons why I should sleep at my residence, I returned to town and passed the night at the hotel.

In the course of the following day I met the sub-sheriff. In conversation with him I mentioned the disappearacce of my horse, which, as I had firmly secured his halter, I was unable to account for. Without a moment's hesitation

the sub-sheriff asserted that the act was probably committed by persons desirous of robbing
me, who considered that on foot I should be
less likely to escape their grasp. In the afternoon I returned to my residence, where, to my
surprise, I learned that the pony had come
home at an early hour, with the halter, not
trailing among his feet, but knotted up to the
saddle bow, a convincing proof that it had been
untied by human hands.

For some evenings afterwards, I did not leave
my home at night, and, as I was alone, paid particular attention to my fire-arms, so that if robbery
were really intended, I should be fully prepared
to give the would-be perpetrators of that crime
a warm reception. To make myself doubly secure
against surprise, I placed one of the terriers in
the hall and took my favourite setter—as watch-
ful an animal as could be desired — into my
bed-room. Nothing, however, occurred to raise
a suspicion that such measures were necessary
for my security. About a week after my horse
had been turned loose, I received an invitation
to visit a gentleman and spend the evening at

his house. As heretofore I rode to the railroad bridge, and secured my mount with more than usual attention, but on my return he was again gone, As I had been detained longer than usual at my friend's residence, it appeared to me more than probable that if I returned to town the hotel would be closed, and therefore, in preference to being locked out, I resolved to reach my own dwelling. Drawing my revolver and cocking it, I pushed rapidly along the road, carefully avoiding such places as might harbour an assailant.

The night was very dark, and a heavy shower which had just fallen prevented my footsteps being heard by any one distant more than a few paces. In due course of time I arrived at a place where the road was fringed with timber and brush-wood on both sides, more particularly next the river. Both my eyes and ears were here of course on the *qui vive*, and my finger touched a trigger that required but slight pressure to send forth a messenger of death. As I stole noiselessly along, a sound which was indistinct at first, but which afterwards became so audible that I plainly recognized it as the voice of a man arguing with listeners, struck upon my ear. I halted, and placing my ear to the ground, listened. "Not coming," I heard a voice say, in evident allusion to my delay. I therefore crossed the fence, struck over the meadow, and reached my residence in safety. Calling up my servant, I dispatched him for Kelly. The plucky fellow, without a moment's hesitation, answered my summons. With my man and him for companions, each armed with a six-shooter, I started down the road in the opposite direction, hoping to surprise the ambuscade which I most thoroughly believed to be laid for me.

We were unsuccessful, however, for although we used every precaution, onr approach became known, and the supposed highwaymen beat their retreat to a boat which we discovered through the darkness floating upon the placid bosom of the river, but in which not a single figure could be distinguished. The occupants were doubtless stretched upon the bottom, to avoid the chance of being turned into targets.

I had every reason to congratulate myself that Providence had, in circumstances of such danger, taken me under his sheltering wing; for the men who would have robbed me in the silence of night, would scarcely have hesitated to take my life with the view of securing their own safety. The old adage, " Dead men tell no tales," is as well known in America as in other lands. As it was impossible to remain always tied to the house, the above warning made me doubly particular in keeping my fire-arms in a fit state for immediate use. Thank goodness, however, I have not yet been called upon to use them.

A visitor from Cincinnati, who has been residing with me for a few days, being anxious before his return home to enjoy some fishing, I despatched a waggon for a boat, as the pond at the back of the farm was the intended scene of operations. My messenger, after a long search, succeeded in obtaining one, but, before it could be trusted on the water, hours had to be spent caulking it, and even then it leaked so much that an incessant baling had to be kept up. Our bait was minnow, of which we had obtained an abundant supply.

For the first few hours, until the cool of evening set in, little success rewarded our efforts. At length, however, the fish commenced to remark our baits, and they attacked them with such ravenous appetites that we were several times on the verge of sinking, from neglecting to employ our baling dish. At the time when our bait was nearly exhausted, we had not succeeded in capturing anything over six or seven pounds in weight. In fact we had reached the fag-end of our minnows, and were contemplating the cessation of our labours, when my friend's float suddenly disappeared, and the strain upon his line was so severe that the rod was bent double. A prize worthy of the exercise of all skill and patience was now beyond doubt hooked.

My companion was a little nervous man, and his excitement was so great that I every moment feared he would be guilty of some indiscretion that would lose him his prize. His pipe, in the first place, fell out of his mouth, and to save it from the water he left go his rod with one hand, and snatched wildly at his pipe with the other. The jerk which this movement produced upon the rod, recalled the fish to a consciousness of the danger of its position, and off it darted with a rush, which did not cease till every yard of line was run off the reel, where it parted. So far neither of us had seen the prey, and were therefore ignorant of its species. I had a surmise, however, which afterwards turned out to be correct.

With disappointment stamped on every feature of his face, and careless whether we floated or swamped, my friend sat down in the bottom of the boat, and bemoaned the fate which had treated him so scurvily. He was inconsolable. No amount of condolence would comfort him. Such a chance of taking a leviathan might never occur again. Although I might have been of the same opinion, I did not express my thought, but endeavoured to administer balm to his wounded feelings. While thus engaged I observed, not over fifty yards from our position, the float my companion had lost sailing along the surface, end on, at such a rate of velocity that its capture in our water-logged boat would require an unusual amount of promptitude and exertion. Out went the oars. The sculls one sees in a Thames wherry, or on board a man-of-war's boat, would feel insulted if they heard such a name applied to the things that I laid hold of. If, however, we did not mean to give up all hope of overtaking the float, it was necessary to employ them. A heavy old lumbering boat, when free from water, is not the lightest craft to handle, but that in which we were had not less than a foot of water in it, and it evinced an evident tendency to turn upside down. Grasping my oars, I got seated amidships after a great deal of finessing, and with a long and strong stroke started in pursuit. I tugged and pulled till I thought my heart would burst, but all my exertions did not appear to bring us any nearer to the prize. Things, however, at length improved, and the prospect of success looked more probable, for the cork had attached itself to some floating reeds which lay in its track.

Losing no time, I renewed my efforts, convinced that three or four strokes would now do the work. Dipping my blade deep, I soon had the satisfaction of shooting alongside the float; but every effort to catch it with my gaff failed, and tired, disheartened, and disgusted, I was about to give up, when a portion of the line a few yards above the float was secured, and I had the satisfaction of discovering that the prize was still attached to the hook. I played the fish very cautiously, giving and taking line as circumstances suggested. I was not permitted, however, to do this without interruption from my companion, who reminded me that the fish was on his hook, and that he consequently should have the honour of completing the capture. If, however, I succeeded in securing it, he should still consider the fish his, and in talking of the matter with his friends should not dream of giving me any credit in the affair. I did not care much so that we succeeded; nor did I attempt to argue with him, but kept possession of the line.

At length time and strain operated so effec-

tually as to reduce the strength of the fish,
and inch by inch I coaxed him nearer the surface. O shades of night! what a splendid
fellow he was! I will not say how long,
because fishermen measuring with the eye are
never believed. I coaxed the pike nearer and
nearer to the boat's gunwale, which it approached slowly and unwillingly. A few feet
more, and it would be close enough to gaff.
The moment that required to be done my companion took the implement into his hand, and
I whispered to him a word of caution that he
should not be in a hurry—but you cannot
get men on such occasions to attend to advice.
Disregarding all I had said, with a half thrust
and half jerk he made a scoop at the fish,
and the impetuosity of his movement so nearly
capsized the boat that she took buckets of
water over her side, and so terrified the pike
that, with a swirl of the tail, it started from
us, the hook breaking at the bend with the
suddenness of the strain.

Of course, my friend blamed me, and I blamed
him. The points in reference to the case were

argued again and again, and every time each
became more positive in support of his own
position. We at length reached shore, drenched
like two water-spaniels, and neither of us in the
sweetest of tempers.

The variety and quantity of fish in this pond
are great, and many of them attain considerable
magnitude. Originally, no doubt, they came
from the Wabash, when the country was flooded,
for I do not believe that, in a spot so contracted, and containing so many inhabitants,
spawn would ever be permitted to become mature.

On the side next the high ground, where
some alder bushes grow in the water, I have
seen on a very warm and bright day such
numbers of water-vipers twined round the
limbs and trunks which margin the pond that
it would be almost impossible to wade a yard
without being within reach of one of them.
They certainly have all the appearance of being
venomous, for their heads are obtuse, large, and
wide, while their bodies are very short in proportion to their thickness. The inhabitants,

however, say they are harmless. They feed principally on fish, frogs, and small birds. The latter they obtain by climbing to the upper limbs of trees and robbing the nests. Turtles also abound here, and if a plank or log were left floating on the surface for a few hours, every vacant spot upon its surface would become occupied by one of these amphibii.

The large turtles are excellent for the table, but are difficult to obtain. Attempting to shoot them is useless, for even supposing you drill a hole through them, they always manage to gain the bottom, where they secrete themselves. Their eggs, however, are frequently found, and form at all times an agreeable addition to the *cuisine.*

For some time preparations have been making for a crop of tobacco. Divine tobacco! those that know you appreciate your worth. Of late years how rapidly have you increased in popularity, a proof that the longer you are known the less can be said against you, the more urged in your favour. But I daresay there are hundreds that smoke their pipes and cigars—gazing, day after day, into the circling volumes of smoke they are sending forth—who enjoy the soothing influence of the Nicotian weed in all its perfection, yet do not know how their favourite leaf is cultivated. My experience on the subject was gained practically, and although my essay as a tobacco-grower was not remarkable for success, still I believe I learned sufficient to justify me in supposing that, if ever again I should have the same facilities and desire to re-embark in a second speculation, I should be able to give to the world different results.

On the farm, as I have previously stated, was a considerable extent of hilly ground, which, until the Winter, retained its covering of virgin timber. Harris, who had become installed as overseer, had spent all his early days in a portion of Kentucky where much attention was devoted to tobacco-culture. Of course, under such circumstances, it may naturally be expected that he is accepted here as quite an authority on this subject. From observations he has made in his wanderings about the estate, he has long come to the conclusion that there never was a farm better suited for raising a tobacco crop than my present home. In his opinion, Indian corn, barley, or stock will never yield such profits as are to be derived from the cultivation of tobacco. In fact, he has almost got us to believe that we have but to sow, to reap a hundred-fold.

Every person is fond of making money, and Harris appears so earnest and sincere, as well as sanguine, that my landlord and myself have become converts to his ideas. Not to be guilty of rashness, however, sundry authorities have been consulted, and the more the matter is considered, the more feasible appears the undertaking. We ultimately determine, therefore, to sink a considerable sum of money in what appears destined to bring us in a large amount of remuneration.

The preparations which must be made in order to obtain a maiden crop of tobacco are as follow:

"The timber must, in the first place, be cleared off the land, and such trees as are without value for fencing, shingles, or building purposes are cut into cord-wood for firing, the sale of which will indemnify for this portion of the outlay, possibly leaving a considerable profit. The ground then requires to be under-brushed, the *débris* being gathered into heaps, which have to be consumed with fire. The ashes that remain are then scattered over the soil, previous to the earth being broken up. This is comparatively easy work, and, provided sufficient hands can be obtained, so far all is plain-sailing. The next operation, however, that of ploughing, is much more difficult.

In a meadow, or open prairie, this part of the preparatory work might be easily accomplished, but, on ground lately denuded of timber, roots, and stumps are so numerous that much patience and great perseverance are necessary to perform the task properly. The soil being ready, the tobacco-plants, which have been previously raised in a hot-bed, after the manner of young celery, are placed in it at regular intervals of four or five feet. The sooner they are got into the ground the better, but, at the same time, it must be remembered that one night of frost would destroy the result of all our labour. For this reason it is generally thought necessary to retain a supply of surplus plants, to replace those that may thus be unfortunately lost.

After the tobacco has attained the size of a large lettuce it is topped, that is, the upper extremity of the main stem is broken off so as to throw all the strength of growth into the leaves, which are reduced to four in number. At this period, and till the tobacco becomes ripe, it is requisite to take the greatest possible care that the tobacco-worm does not obtain a footing in the plant, it being so destructive, that in a few days it will reduce every plant to nothing but fibres. To prevent such a misfortune, persons must daily go over the field, examining each leaf in rotation, and carefully clearing them of this noxious grub. Where a tobacco field is enclosed, it is no uncommon thing to make turkeys perform this work, but they have to be half-starved and shut in, or they will not do their labour effectively. However fond they may be of tobacco-worms, they appear to act upon the principle of the old adage : " Enough is as good as a feast." Fancy our being fed on nothing but shrimps for weeks together. However much we liked them previously, they would doubtless ever afterward be looked upon with aversion.

In course of time the leaves commence to assume a golden tinge, an indication that the crop is fit for the sickle. It is then cut and hung in barns constructed for the purpose, when in time it becomes cured. Of course, all of us have seen some very bright-coloured golden tobacco. This attractive appearance is produced artificially, by burning dead, damp wood underneath the plants as they hang in the barn. Before going to market it is sorted over, similar qualities and leaves equal in size being tied together in what are called "hands." The price varies according to quality, of which there may not unfrequently be varieties in different parts of the same field; one portion selling for over a dollar, the other for less than five cents per pound.

The season thus far has been favourable,

and our hopes of success are more than sanguine.

Having heard that the locomotive on the railroad (for the Ohio and Mississippi line passed
within a mile of my residence) had killed one
of our milk-cattle, I went over to investigate
the matter, and assemble a board of the neighbours to appraise its value, supposing I found
the report to be true. This is the course
always followed, and their finding will be sup-
ported by the county authorities. The railroad
monopolists, however, will often give those
having claims against them much trouble before
payment of the money, particularly if they
suppose they have been over-charged. I am
glad to say that on this occasion I was not
called upon to make a charge against their
finances.

While walking along the railroad, under the
telegraph wires, I found a brace of Prairie
chickens which had just been killed. As I have
several times before had the same fortune, my
brain was set to work to discover what could be
the cause of their death. After mature con-

sideration, I have come to the conclusion that they met their fate from flying against the wires. Kelly, the section-master of this portion of the track, informed me that, after a severe gale of wind in the Autumn of last year, he picked up three wild geese which had doubtless met their fate in a similar manner. I doubt if our pheasants and partridges at home are ever guilty of similar recklessness of life and disregard of consequences. I am informed, however, by an intelligent friend and naturalist that such casualties are not uncommon in England, especially when the telegraph wires are newly set up, and that, in particular, members of the thrush tribe are frequently so killed. My friend has had several instances within his own observation, and a relative of his, past whose garden telegraphic wires stretched, used to go every morning in search of the previous night's victims.

CHAPTER V.

Mount Carmel—A Long Delayed Trip—On the Bosom of the Wabash—Timber on the Banks of the River—Haunts for Elfins—Wary Turtle—The Wood-duck—Turkey-Buzzards—Is a Turtle a Fish?—Skilful Angling—Ball at a Farmer's House—"Go it, Britisher."—Republican Freedom—Slough of Despond—The Snake Fence—A Charge of Hogs.

ABOUT twenty miles by land, and double that distance by water, on a bend of the Wabash, to the east, is situated Mount Carmel. In the old times, when Iroquois and Chippewas owned the country, before the forest had given place to clearings and the Prairie grass was cropped by domestic cattle, there was a rapid ford here, and many are the grand pow-wows and war-party meetings of Red-skins that took place where now reposes this quiet and diminutive village.

To assist the navigation of the river and facilitate the ascent and descent of large craft, a dam has been thrown across where the rapids existed, and an extensive lock constructed. The consequence is that all the migratory fish when returning north from the lower rivers lodge, if there should be a scarcity of water, underneath this dam, when at certain seasons of the year the angler can catch such numbers of them, of different varieties, as must delight the heart of the most covetous sportsman. For a week or two a visit to Mount Carmel has been discussed, but nothing definite arranged. In fact it almost looked as if the whole affair were tumbling through, when the arrival of some friends who were passionately fond of angling led to the determination to undertake our long procrastinated trip. In the neighbourhood both my landlord and myself knew several nice girls, and to make the excursion more enjoyable we determined to charter a small steam-boat then lying at Vincennes, invite the young ladies and their aunts, or guardian relations, thus increasing our numbers to fifteen or sixteen, and make our stay at Mount Carmel as long as we found the place agreeable and the fishing good.

As soon as it became public on what a grand scale our excursion was to be conducted, invitations rose to a premium, and we might have quadrupled the number of excursionists without the least trouble. Knowing, however, how much depends upon a company of this description being kept select, we preferred braving the wrath of the disappointed to risking the chance of having the pleasure of our excursion marred.

The two days previous to our start were spent in attending to the commissariat department, and every delicacy that could be procured from my Vincennes grocer, ranging from French *pâtés* to Indian curries, and from Spanish sherries to German still wines, were stored away in sufficient quantities to meet every emergency. At length the looked for hour of departure arrived, and in the presence of a crowd who had assembled to see us off, the gangway was drawn in, the painter unhooked, and the paddle commenced to revolve.

A cheer from the shore bid us good speed, and we were free on the bosom of the Wabash.

To those who have not had the fortune to float upon an American river, a word or two descriptive of its appearance may not be inappropriate, more especially as all the streams of this continent, situated between the latitude of our present position and the Gulf of Mexico, are very much alike in general characteristics. This is accounted for by the fact that the country is unmarked by elevated grounds, and that the soil, especially on the river banks, is of that rich black loam which is formed through the deposit for successive years of alluvial refuse.

The timber, as might be expected, deserves more than a passing remark, for it possesses the proportions with which the tropics are accredited, with the brilliant and healthful colouring of that of the temperate zone. The elm, sycamore, and yellow poplar are probably most numerously represented here, while the Catalpa and walnut are not unfrequent. Another tree, not very abundant, but well known further south, is the cotton-wood, which often grows to the most gigantic proportions and forms a prominent object in every southern landscape where timber is introduced. Peering from the deck of the steam-boat into the dark shady retreats, for ever isolated from the sun's rays by the thick upper screen of impenetrable foliage, the romantic and imaginative naturally exclaim, What a place for elfins, sprites, and water-nymphs to haunt! But Banshees and Lurlines not having yet taken to emigration, the only thing we observe that has any tendency to create a belief in the supernatural is the erratic will-o'-the-wisp of which we have an occasional glance.

In the middle of the stream, and hanging to the bank are numerous partially-decayed trees of immense proportions, whose existence had been cut short either through the sweeping whirl-wind or the insidious sapping of the water beneath. They lie in every direction, sometimes piled on each other, like soldiers who have succumbed sticking to their colours in the thickest of the fight. On such of those prostrate trunks as lie in the water, numerous turtles will be observed asleep; but they are wondrously wary, and can only be approached closely by one moving with the greatest stealth and silence. I have always regarded them with great curiosity, their habits and modes of life being still enshrouded in much mystery. In the Wabash, to my certain knowledge, there are four distinct species, so much resembling each other as to be generally taken for one and the same, while the fourth and largest, instead of being encased in hard armour, is protected by a covering more pliable than, and not at all unlike to sole-leather.

The American wood-duck, a far more lovely child of nature, is noted for its affection to its young. We observed, with the greatest interest, her anxiety to keep her defenceless brood beyond our reach. She swam first with her head on one side, then on the other, the better to mark every movement that seemed to indicate hostility to her children. Every American is proud of this bird, for it is only found in their land. One peculiarity possessed by it is that it rests only on trees, and builds its nest in them.

We pursued our course at a velocity of eight or ten knots an hour, passing some dark miasmatic-looking streams. The navigation is made intricate in some places by bars and sandbanks. Here and there snags protrude their heads, like leviathan snakes, over the surface of the water. Yet the dark sombre wall of gigantic trees remains unbroken, while the stillness that reigns over all is disturbed only by the heavy human-like breathing of our steam-power. In turning an abrupt corner of the stream, we surprised a large party of turkey-buzzards. With the utmost speed they could command, they attempted awkwardly to take wing. A few succeeded, while the more indolent or over-gorged, satisfying themselves that danger was not to be apprehended, sat still, staring with their bleared goggle eyes at the intruders. A close examination of the vicinity disclosed a dead stag—his horns still perfect, although the carcass was much disfigured and decayed. Was age the cause of his decease, or, what was more probable,

had he received his death-wound from the hand
of man? At length the river commenced to
widen, the greater sluggishness of the current
plainly telling of increased depth. To the left
we saw an opening in the timber, which gradually appeared to increase in magnitude as we
approached it, till suddenly we were rewarded by
a view of several snow-white houses, with bright
green blinds, the abodes evidently of comfort and
prosperity. These formed Mount Carmel.

That afternoon all commenced fishing, the
ladies vying with the rougher sex in capturing
the silver-scaled tenants of the stream. It had
been settled among us that, however large any
fish, our fair friends were to receive no assistance from their male escort till it was fairly
landed. This arrangement created a diversity of
opinion sooner than might have been expected;
for the youngest of our party, who was also its
greatest beauty, had scarcely got her line into
the water when she felt a most decided bite.
She struck with courage, and the hook went
home. How her rod bent as she employed all
her strength to bring her prize to the surface!

By degrees, but very slowly, she was accomplishing her object, when to our intense merriment,
a turtle, and not a fish, turned out to be the
captive. The question, however, arose, was a
turtle a fish? Not being consulted on the subject, I did not offer an opinion, but listened to
the *pros* and *cons* of the discussion that ensued.
At length it was decided that Mr. —— might
land the prize, provided that if turtle was
proved to be a fish he should stand champagne.
Mr. —— was " spoony " on this young lady,
and would have paid for " Imperial Tokay "
all round for one sweet smile. We all enjoyed
ourselves ; mosquitos were the only drawback,
exhibiting a marked preference for our fair
friends. If I were a mosquito I really think I
should do the same.

Well, we caught fish in great variety till we
were tired, several of them remarkable in size.
Thoroughly satisfied with our excursion, on the
fourth day we started on our return journey.
One result of our expedition was neither more
nor less than a double wedding. The young
ladies, it is evident, had not fished in vain,

when two gentlemen, supposed to be confirmed bachelors, got hooked.

On my arrival at home I found an invitation to a ball at the house of a farmer, who cultivated extensively in the neighbourhood, awaiting me. Of course I accepted, particularly as the affair did not come off for a couple of days, as I felt convinced I should have an insight into life that would afford me much amusement. The host, who was well to do in the world, and possessed considerable local political interest, had a son, whom he had succeeded in getting appointed to a lieutenancy in one of the volunteer regiments; and before the young aspirant for military glory joined his corps, the worthy sire had determined to do the hospitable, by throwing open his house. Resolved to be punctual, I arrived at my destination at the moment when they were organizing the first dance. If I had been half-an-hour late, it would have been considered a great mark of disrespect. How different is this from London!

The weather for the two previous days had been excessively wet, and when it rains here it does so to such purpose that the surface of the country becomes so saturated as to make it resemble an immense sponge. Patent leather boots, therefore, did not figure on the feet of the performers on the light and fantastic toe—but the heaviest cow-skins. It was a funny scene. The dignity ball of Jamaica, so admirably described by Captain Marryatt, is the nearest approach to it that I can at present recall.

On a table in a corner sat the fiddler, a personage evidently of great importance in his own estimation. From his instrument he produced the most doleful sounds, and before each figure sung out with a broad nasal twang directions to the dancers. In his cheek was an immense quid of tobacco, which imparted to his physiognomy a distortion similar to that seen in persons suffering from gumboil, or in the monkeys at the Zoological, with an unusual quantity of dainties stowed away in their jaws for future consumption. The Emperor of Russia is no doubt a great man in his own dominions, but he could not be a greater autocrat than this fiddler, who actually bullied the Parson when he attempted to ask him a question; and it requires a big man to do that in this great country. The ladies were all very prim and stiff, and the gentlemen no less formal. Their display of courtly manner partook in some measure of the antique. I could almost fancy that I had gone back three centuries in the age of the world, when I was recalled abruptly to a sense of my present position by the query sharply and emphatically delivered by the violinist.

"Mister Britisher, ain't you larned yet how to dance? Buckle to, and give us an old country step." All eyes were at once fixed on me, and my reputation depended upon my compliance. I would have given a fiver to be out of the mess, but such liberality would not have saved me. So I "buckled to" with a partner, wizened as a mummy, with only three teeth visible to do duty for a mouthful. This lady seemed to think that on her lasting powers, and the number of antics she performed, depended her chance of obtaining a husband.

I had learned in my infancy to dance a Scottish reel; at one period I had no slight knowledge of the Highland fling, and had also paid a man of the dancing-master breed, I cannot say how much, to teach me a hornpipe that was necessary in a *rôle* I was about to enact at a theatrical performance given by amateurs. So I jumbled them all up together, first trying one step and then another, and as I was in good condition I kept it up with all the energy I could command. The result was that I established my reputation as a master of the Terpsichorean art, and from that moment forth all eyes in that goodly assembly looked upon me as an authority on it. "Go it, Britisher!" I heard several times exclaimed, and—"I went it."

Among the ladies that graced with their presence this ever to be remembered occasion was a fresh, pleasant girl, rather dairy-maid in style. For her smiles there were two rivals, the young lieutenant and a late arrival in the room, whom I recognised as a German shoemaker that lived some miles off. Before the appearance of the latter, the son of Mars had had it all his own way, and evidently was availing himself of every opportunity to gain a hold on the feelings of the object of his adoration; but after the arrival of the shoemaker he found a rival whose chances of winning the race were at a premium. After greeting all friends, he of the last and waxed end sat down in a corner, deliberately kicked off his dirty boots, pulled from his pocket a pair of clean socks, which he put on *over* those he had previously worn, and, with the air of one who is conscious of perfect familiarity with the laws of etiquette, produced a pair of pumps, in which he deliberately encased his feet. When he had completed his toilette, the fair one, who had been observing all his movements, approved, with numerous gracious smiles, his excessive ideas of gentility. The poor lieutenant was from this time forth vanquished; his hilarity had departed, and his visage perceptibly lengthened.

But the "wee small hours" rolled rapidly on, and increased in magnitude till day commenced to break, and with it the assembly to disperse. My horse was already at the door, and I was only delaying my departure to get an opportunity to thank the host for the enjoyment he had afforded, when a disturbance arose in the room. The shoe-maker's boots had been purloined! Who was the thief? No one could say. My suspicions immediately pointed to the officer in the army. But the wrangling did not long continue, for a shrill voice called into the room "Philip" (that was the German's name) "if you be coming you had better look spry."

"But I can't find my boots," answered the shoe-maker.

"Well, I'm off without you, you had best come as you are," responded the lady.

Ten minutes afterwards I passed the lovers on the road. The leader of the *bon ton* was looking, by the uncertain grey light of dawn, for one of his pumps 'which had been drawn off his foot by the mud. I scarcely envied him his bootless tramp of four long miles. Well done the young soldier! thought I, you have saved the reputation of your profession in *affaires du cœur*, by stealing so clever a march upon the enemy.

At the back of my residence was situated a dense brake of red-wood, dog-wood, and brush-hazel. Farther off still and on its margin lay a swamp, which certainly was not large, but although curtailed in extent, was as admirable a specimen of these American damp, dark, and loathsome morasses as the most fastidious hater of pestilential places could shudder at. Although there were no alligators or other large amphibians to be found within its limits, yet the person who had the hardihood to traverse it could discover, without any great effort of search, rattle-snakes, copper-heads, and adders in tolerable abundance. Generally speaking, I accorded this sequestered retreat a wide berth, and certainly always did so from choice. Occasionally, however, a cow, sheep, or horse would stray within its limits, and I was compelled to seek the truants or run the risk of their loss.

Within a few hundred yards of this " slough of despond "—for by this name I knew it—was situated a field of Indian corn on the cultivation of which I had expended a considerable sum ; and, from the soil being rich and the weather propitious, the probability was that in due season I should receive ample returns for my outlay.

To the farmer the prospect of a good crop is
always agreeable, and day after day I calculated
with the most intense satisfaction how many
bushels per acre would "be the probable yield—
how many dollars and cents, in fact, would be
returned to my pocket, as profit on this speculation. Weeds grow unsolicited almost anywhere.
If the soil is rich, they come forth and flourish
with a luxuriance that is most provoking. In
fields of Indian corn, especially when they are
on low rich meadow grounds, the cockle-burr
and morning-glory will, unless hoeing and
ploughing are resorted to, rapidly usurp the
place of the crop, killing by their embrace and
vicinity the less hardy plants that produce the
staff of life.

Knowing this, I traversed my field of maize
with the intention of learning on what portion
it would be judicious for the operation of
weeding to commence, and had almost settled
the doubtful point when I discovered an open
verge of the timber land so rooted up, trampled
down, and otherwise destroyed, that without a
moment's hesitation I concluded that cattle or

hogs, belonging either to myself or neighbours, were in the habit of resorting here to gratify their appetites in the most unrestrained manner.

Now, if such incursions were allowed to continue, in a month or less there would not remain a stem, much less a head of corn, in a field that promised to produce an unusually large yield. With this fact staring me in the face, I instituted a search along the fence and at last found where the depredators had forced an entrance. Walls and hedges were scarcely known in the locality of which I write. The snake-fence, peculiarly an American institution, is here universally in use. It is easily erected, and with as much facility pulled down; and as the successful farmer on the Western Continent has to put his shoulder to the wheel, I stripped off my coat without hesitation and commenced reconstructing the tumbled-down parts of the encircling rails.

I had been thus occupied only a short time when an angry grunt informed me that some specimen of life was in the vicinity. I peered again and again into the dark labyrinth of trees and underbush, but was unable to detect the creature from whom these expressive sounds proceeded. There being no animals *feræ naturæ* in the neighbourhood, I was not in the least alarmed. Curiosity alone might prompt a desire to become acquainted with the individual to whom I was indebted for the salutation. But my labour was completed, and I was about to depart when a movement in the bush attracted my attention, although from impediments intervening I could not obtain a fair view. At length, however, I was thoroughly startled by a crushing of underbrush and a crackling of dead sticks, and perceived to my surprise, three, four, yes, half-a-dozen immense hogs charging down upon me. There was no time for thought or hesitation, so I instantly turned on my heel and made, as the Americans say, " tracks " to the nearest object that promised me shelter. The race was short, but, considering its brevity unusually severe.

The vantage I sought was a charred stump, five feet or more high, and when I gained it the first and second effort failed to place me on its summit. If unsuccessful in another struggle to gain the top of the perch, I should be too late to put into execution any other *ruse* that might occur to my mind, for already the pursuers were within a few yards of my person. With a desperate effort I exerted all my physical strength, and the urgency of the case giving me unwonted power, I obtained an uncertain, nervous and trembling footing upon the summit of my sanctuary, and turning round to face my antagonists I thanked my stars that such was the case, for in manners and appearance they were most unpolite and ferocious.

Fancy being perched like a bear at the Zoo on the top of a pole, with a herd of vicious porkers expressing, in their guttural and most unmusical dialect, their hope and desire for your speedy fall into the midst of them! It may be intensely comic to read of, but to me, the principal in the drama, it was sensationally tragico-grotesque.

The position of an owl that circumstances have compelled to perch out in the open, and

which is assailed by every insignificant bird from
the chattering magpie to the diminutive oriole
fly-catcher, was very similar to mine. Previous
to the occurrence of this little *contretemps*, I
should have laughed at Minerva's favourite being
subjected to such persecutions, but sympathy,
from personal experience of a similar fate, would
now induce me to go to his relief. We can com-
passionate the misfortunes of others when we
have had a taste of similar treatment ourselves.
The charity of the poor towards each other can
thus be accounted for, for they have tasted the
bitter draught of adversity, and feel for those
that have to endure it.

Those persons who have never strayed beyond
city homes and watering-place retreats may
smile at the idea of any one trembling before
half-a-dozen pigs; but they only see in imagination well-fed, chubby porkers, with small ears
and expanded cheeks, which sleep two-thirds of
their time, and find the exercise of walking from
their dormitory to their trough as much as they
can accomplish with comfort. The animals I
had to do with were as dissimilar from their do-

mesticated brethren as the gaunt grey wolf is from my lady's lap-dog.

Few persons do not know how trees are felled in America; but I may inform those who are ignorant of the process that an immense wedge is cut out of either side with the axe, thus leaving on the stump a sharp comb, or ridge, far from the most agreeable surface to rest upon for those accustomed to chairs, sofas, and beds.

Ten minutes' confinement on such a perch was severe punishment, and double the time rendered the suffering almost unendurable. My custodians, however, would not depart, and did not show the slightest intention of doing so. Round and round the stump they snuffed and rooted, while their little eyes, gleaming with a malicious twinkle, were kept fixed upon me. If I stirred to ease any portion of my frame which was beginning to suffer from cramp, the whole fraternity would rush together close to my roosting place. One old fellow among them several times showed an inclination to attempt mounting the stump and taking my citadel by assault, but was dissuaded by a kick from my heavy cow-skin boot.

How long I should have been detained there goodness only knows. What torment I might have suffered I cannot imagine, but this I am certain of, that never was an unskilled rider more fearfully galled by a hard-trotting horse than your humble servant when released from his exalted position.

But " there's a sweet little cherub that sits up aloft," and on this occasion I was wonderfully favoured; for some of the labourers of a neighbouring farm, on the search for missing cattle, passed by, and my shouts attracting their attention, they came to my rescue. My adventure created much laughter when it became known, and I was chaffed unmercifully—sly allusions being made to my love of pork, or to a veteran in arms being ignominiously routed by half-a-dozen pigs.

I determined, however, to be revenged, and as these hogs were evidently no person's property, was only to be satisfied with blood. I resolved, therefore, to invite all my acquaintances in the neighbourhood, who thought they could ride, and were partial to a lark, to join me at breakfast next day, after which I intended to provide them with a run of a novel character, that would be certain to produce an immensity of fun.

Perhaps I was the more disposed to this procedure, that I had in my time done not a little "pig-sticking" in the plains of India, and might have an opportunity to restore to pristine brightness those laurels which, in my neighbours' eyes, were somewhat tarnished by my adventure upon that abominable and never-to-be-forgotten stump. Yet it was a friend in need, and why should I malign it now?

CHAPTER VI.

FOR days the fish that had escaped my friend
and myself had not been forgotten, and the
most uncontrollable desire had obtained possession of me to make an essay for its capture.
Kelly's son, therefore, was employed to obtain
me a kettle of minnows. This the boy succeeded
in doing to my satisfaction, and I reached the
pond in the afternoon about the hour when the fish
on my previous visit had commenced to feed.
Being alone I anticipated success. How is it
that, when such is the case, the result is always

greater than was expected? Possibly because, like old women, when we have company we must always be magging.

With little difficulty I got the boat to the proper anchorage, and soon after commenced fishing. It was evident that I was that day in luck's way; for scarcely had my float rested on the water 'when it went under, and a fine black-bass was taken. Again the same operation was repeated, with this difference that a cat-fish was my prize. After an hour and a-half, I might have rested satisfied, but that the mammoth of the pool had not put in an appearance. Again and again several smaller fish were taken, and the time sped so rapidly that I had thoughts of retiring, when my float went down lightly, and then returned to the surface, where it remained for some moments motionless. At length there was a perceptible strain upon it, and from horizontal it became perpendicular. It dipped gradually and slowly deeper in the water, and at length disappearing under the surface with a rush, I struck strongly, and my reward was the discovery that I was fast to a large fish. His first run was splendid, but after it was over the "cur" became apparent in his submissive manner, and his want of energy in resisting his capture. Using my gaff, I at length succeeded in bringing the prize safely into the boat. Although this pike weighed twenty-three pounds, I do not think it was as large as the one that escaped on my previous visit to the pond. .   •

It was a beautiful morning, when upwards of a dozen persons, all of whom had just risen from a sumptuous breakfast, made their appearance from my dwelling to select spears from a number which had been hurriedly manufactured for the present occasion. My guests were the *élite* of the hunting community, whose assistance I had obtained to punish the hogs that had treated me with such discourtesy. In the West, except among the Indians, spears were unknown, but knowing how effectually they are handled by my countrymen on the plains of India, and considering them better suited for the present purpose than fire-arms, I insisted that all who joined in the anticipated sport should permit me to dictate the choice of the weapons to be employed.

With many a laugh, grimace, and repartee, all were at last suited, the horses were brought forth and mounted, and without further loss of time we pushed forward to the scene of operations,

First one cover and then another was searched without discovering our quarry. Again and again new places were proposed and inspected without better results, and our campaign began to look as if destined to failure. Where could the brutes have gone? Could a warning voice of danger have admonished them that the locality was dangerous? It certainly seemed so. At last one of the party who knew the country well proposed that the swamp should be examined. With the mud and stagnant water of which it consisted, it was just such a place as hogs (which are supposed to have rather a partiality for poisonous snakes) would select for a wallow. Thither consequently we directed our steps, taking care to "drive" with our party well from the spread out timber towards the prairie.

A look-out whom we had sent on a détour to our front, so as to command a view of the open ground, was instructed to inform us if the game broke cover, by singing out as lustily as his powers would permit the view-hallo.

It was fortunate this precaution had been taken, for ere we had half penetrated through the damp sombre retreat, our ears were greeted with a welcome warning that our search had not been in vain. Hurrying to the front, as rapidly as the clammy adhesive ground would permit without taking too much out of our steeds, we all rallied around the look-out, from whom the welcome signal proceeded; and we were not a moment too soon, for already the game had gained a considerable distance and were going off at a pace which promised to make a long pursuit necessary before we could hope to blood our weapons.

The line of country chosen by the hogs was all that we could desire, for it was firm and well fitted for a gallop. We had, however, to be up and doing, for it was evident that the pigs knew the country well, and were directing their steps for an extensive swamp which, if they gained it without being headed, would be certain to afford them the most ample security.

Holding our horses, therefore, well in hand, off we started. What a scurry of a race it was! Could a crack Melton-Mowbray fox-hunter have witnessed the scene, he would never have forgotten it—for what riders were the party composed of? There were short men, and tall men, fat men and thin men, young and old, the only striking features in common being that all were equally deficient in knowledge of equitation. And goodness, how the spears were in the way! Not one member of the chase appeared able to carry his comfortably. Nor is this to be wondered at, when it is known that there were very few who had not as much to do as lay in their power to prevent them becoming acquainted with mother earth on the shortest notice. Nevertheless, none of the debutants in pig-sticking came to grief, with the exception of a shopkeeper from the neighbouring town, and he certainly got such a spill as must have left an indelible impression upon the tablets of his memory.

The pace was without doubt excellent, for we

were quickly closing with the pursued, whose exertions plainly told that they were rapidly losing the power to go much further. The horse I bestrode was well-bred, in excellent condition, and accustomed to frequent breathers. Is it to be wondered at, then, that I led the van of a field which was spun out over a considerable extent? Feeling myself sure of my steed's power of endurance, I called upon him for additional exertions. My summons was promptly answered, and in a moment after I ranged alongside the largest of the hogs. Lowering the point of my weapon in a moment after an opportunity presented itself for a thrust, I used my spear so effectually that I put the grunter completely *hors de combat.*

Turning round, for the purpose of selecting another victim, I found many of my companions engaged with the enemy. There was much rushing to and fro, and many ineffective efforts to accomplish some feat of arms. The scene in fact defied all description.

At length, by sheer mobbing, another victim was stretched lifeless on the grass. The re-

remaining porkers, seizing the opportunity while the attention of all was directed to this second victim, gained the swamp, to which, from the commencement, they had directed their steps. Tony, "the Dutchman" as he was familiarly called, had won imperishable laurels, if his own account were to be believed, for he had drawn first blood and delivered the *coup de grâce.* His account, however, did not tally with that given by another of the party, and a dispute ensued which promised, if prolonged, to end in blows. This, however, was avoided, and all returned home satisfied with the sport they had enjoyed.

Next day a flaming account was published in the local paper, brilliantly descriptive of the whole scene, the editor being one of the votaries of the chaste Diana who had honoured the occasion with his presence.

A week had elapsed after this event, when all the participants in the sport of hog-sticking were served with a summons to appear before the County-court to show cause why they should not pay the sum of twenty-five dollars for having killed two hogs, the property of two Frenchmen, brothers, who lived in the neighbourhood. When the day of trial arrived, the most able legal advisers were engaged by both sides, and the case was argued most ably. The dangerous and ludicrous position I had been placed in was eloquently expatiated upon by our advocate; while the plaintiff's lawyer pointed out the monstrosity of such a proceeding, disgraceful to all connected with it, and resulting in the premeditated destruction of the innocent (?) property of two peaceful citizens.

The representatives of the legal profession got so excited that they became personal in their remarks to each other, and would doubtless have proceeded further if the magistrate had not called them to order, with some hints as to the consequence of a continuance of their unprecedented conduct. Ultimately, as the Frenchmen could not prove ownership of the defunct swine, the case was dismissed, they having to pay costs.

It might have been expected that this would have terminated the affair, but it did not, for on leaving the court a quarrel, in reference to the finding of the magistrate, ensued between one of the plaintiffs and Tony, which resulted in a regular stand-up fight. Long and fierce was the struggle, but the superior strength of the Dutchman knocked Monsieur out of time, to the delight of all lookers on; not the least amused of whom was the representative of justice, who from an elevated position in the Court-house viewed the sparring exhibition with the most evident enjoyment, and even forgot his dignity so far as frequently to advise his favourite belligerent as to the tactics he should pursue! The poor Frenchman was so sadly mauled that when the combatants were separated I very much doubt if any part of his body was fit for further exertion, save his tongue, which continued uttering such volleys of *sacrés* as it would be a hard task to do adequate penance for.

One of the greatest pleasures I enjoy is a stroll along the Wabash of a calm peaceful evening. What food for contemplation is offered to the mind where the glorious productions of the Creator's handiwork are scattered around with the

greatest profusion!   England, home, and friends
are recalled to the memory by numerous objects
in every direction.   Yet although the surrounding scenery has similarities to that of the mother
country, there is a difference which says as
. plainly as possible to the adopted citizen :   This
is not the land of your birth.   If England has her
charms of beautiful scenery, so has America.
The former may be compared to the blonde of the
north, the latter to the brunette of the south.
Both are perfect, only they represent different
types.

In this vicinity, a lethargic dreamy languor
always floated over the atmosphere towards the
hour when the sun approached the western hori-
zon.   Its effect on all animal life appeared to be
the same as on myself, producing a tendency to
repose and making one feel at peace with all the
world.

The scenery on the Wabash, when in its
quiescent state, evolves in my soul feelings of re-
ligion similar to those called forth by the im-
posing grandeur of church or cathedral, while the
lavish display of the Creator's goodness on all

sides awakens in my heart sentiments of the deepest gratitude.

The road from the ferry, after passing my house, followed the course of the river for many miles northward, and the margin of the stream was thickly clothed with vegetation of great beauty and variety. Among the trees by which the banks were adorned were the graceful feathery birch, the stalwart hickory, the rugged oak, the variegated button-wood, the dark stained sumach, and the Virginian creeper; but as we recede from the river the umbrageous elm and the sombre beech tower over their lesser companions as if to afford them protection.

Here and there, through the dense array of trunks would open a glade which not unfrequently disclosed such lovely vistas of river scenery as would hold the admirer of nature spell-bound.

It is seldom these waters are navigated except by the lumber-man, and when a raft is occasionally seen gliding smoothly onward towards its destination, it by no means diminishes the beauty of the landscape, while it reminds us of these lovely lines of Longfellow's :

' And the evening sun, descending,
  Set the clouds on fire with redness ;
  Burned the broad sky, like a prairie,
  Left upon the level water
  One long track and trail of splendour,
  Down whose stream as down a river,
  Westward, westward, Hiawatha
  Sailed into the fiery sunset,
  Sailed into the purple vapours,
  Sailed into the dusk of evening.'

When a boy, nothing afforded me greater pleasure than a walk on a Spring evening through the well-stocked game-preserves of a neighbouring nobleman, more especially if the weather had only just cleared up after a protracted term of wet; for then all animal life was on the move, as if desirous of enjoying to the utmost the delightfully invigorating and inspiring change. The cock-pheasant struts with pompous bearing, or dashes off on resolute wing to invade the sanctuary of rivals. The timid hare steels forth to the open grass or grain field, preferring to run the danger of betraying her presence to her foes, rather than to remain longer in the damp cover or the dark wood. The wild duck, the most timid of all game, steers for the centre of the murmuring river, or fearlessly directs her course for the open lake or pond.

On the banks of the Wabash, the effect upon the wild animals in the dreamy lethargic evening was similar to that which I have noticed in England. At no period did the deer exhibit such freedom from timidity. I have often noted them watching me from a clump of ferns or bunch of briers, their large dreamy soft eyes seeming to ask in plain terms what this intruder wanted in their haunts. What pranks the squirrels would have, chasing and tearing after one another, first up one tree, then down another, springing from limb to limb, passing like meteors through the tree tops, their rapidity of movement being almost incomprehensible.

Returning from the woods to the margin of the stream, we have other opportunities of seeing how the various specimens of the animal creation are affected by atmospheric influences. A ripple

up the stream betrays the presence of a musk-
rat, which in a moment is joined by another,
just ascended from the bottom, where doubtless
he was making a search for fresh-water mussels.
On approaching each other they salute by
sniffing noses, and then start to have a game
of romps.

Meanwhile, a more cautious gentleman, who
can be partly seen behind the root of a tree, has
been closely examining our appearance. If we
remain quiet he will probably come out from
his cover, advancing with cautious step until
the whole of his long body and tail, both
covered with rich brown fur, is presented to
the view. It is a minx, half otter, half ferret
in habits and choice of food, preying on fish
or fowl, and making water or land equally its
home. With the undulating, gliding motion of
the snake it gains the margin and disappears into
the water, without leaving a bubble to mark
the place of its entrance. In a few minutes it
re-appears, seated upon a distant stone, whence it
surveys its position, eagerly examining whether
any game is within reach. Diving once more,

it directs its course towards a brood of wild duck seeking their evening meal among the broad spread lotus leaves. One of the unhappy family will doubtless soon be struggling in the deadly embrace of the minx.

What is that sound of chip! chip! coming repeatedly from that brush heap? It is the chipmonk or hackie, the *Tamias* of America, sitting on the stump of a tree, his golden fur glistening in the rays of the sun, and then, so quick and graceful in his movements, starting off again, showing the broad-pencilled lines along his back as he hops from stump to log. Nearly all over the country these beautiful squirrels, which are very abundant, are alike popular with young and old. The nest is built in the ground, and hoarded in it is the winter stock of provisions. There the ground squirrel sleeps away the dreary season, indifferent alike to rain, storm, or cold.

Three other species of squirrel are also frequently seen here, the black, grey, and fox, all of which, especially the latter, exceed in size our English representative of the race. Being justly esteemed a great delicacy for the table, they are much persecuted. Yet their numbers do not decrease so rapidly as might be expected. In warm weather they remain secreted from the powerful rays of the mid-day sun, but evening brings them forth, full of frolic and mischief.

Topsy and Tip were with me one evening when I had strolled forth to enjoy the holiday-making of the beauties I have attempted to describe. Dog-like, they were peering into every hiding place likely to secrete a fox. Several hares had been started by them, but the timid fleet-footed creatures were too swift for their pursuers, and had almost run the terriers to a stand-still. My attention was attracted by an oriole flying out from a dense growth of the wild grape-vine that closely bound in its arms an aged maple.

Hoping to find the bird's nest I searched carefully, but in vain. In my efforts, however, I disturbed a skunk. The wary animal, conscious of its powers of defence, quietly walked off, as if the idea of pursuit never entered its brain. In this respect it was perfectly right, as far as I was concerned; but my active dogs, with their sharp prying eyes and keen noses, knew neither discretion nor fear.

In a moment Topsy saw the stranger. A sharp bark told her companion of her discovery, and in an instant both dogs were in pursuit. It was not in my power to prevent the catastrophe I dreaded, for ere my voice reached my companions, they had rushed on their prey. In a moment the air was loathsome with the fumes from the fluid discharge, which a skunk emits when in danger. This stench is so strong and disagreeable that persons have been known to faint from its effects. The skunk made a most game struggle for life, and fully five minutes were occupied in accomplishing its death, by which time both the dogs were so thoroughly sprinkled with the disgusting liquid, that it was most disagreeable to come within many yards of them.

Dogs invariably become ill after killing one of these brutes; yet this has not, in my experience, the slightest effect in preventing them from repeating the operation when an opportunity occurs. This is fortunate for the farmer who possesses dogs, however disagreeable it may be to the gentleman owner, for if the dogs were to show the white feather, it would be impossible to raise a head of poultry round a farm-yard. The skunks are so cunning that they seldom can be trapped, and they are so persevering in their search for fowls, their favourite prey, that it is almost impossible to prevent them gaining access, some time or other, to the poultry-house.

Mrs. Kelly, I must inform my readers, had been for a week or two established as house-keeper. Although I was perfectly aware that a more honest little woman never breathed, I was compelled to call her attention to the immense, in fact, I may say impossible consumption of tea, coffee, and sugar that was going on in my house-hold.

The good little woman agreed with me that there must be something wrong. The wants of my family-circle not being equal to the amount used, it was naturally concluded that pilfering must be taking place; but who the robbers were, neither her shrewdness nor mine could imagine. This morning, however, the thieves were discovered by my employée.

It happened in this way. The little woman, having business which would occupy the greater portion of the day to attend to in town, rose at an unusually early hour to enable her to perform all her home duties before leaving. On entering my kitchen, the girls of Harris were discovered in the act of helping themselves · to the groceries.

So thoroughly were they prepared for the task that each was provided with a can in which to stow away the pilfered articles, At breakfast I was informed of this circumstance; and as I met the children immediately afterwards when enjoying my morning pipe, I gave each a severe scolding and forbade them ever in future to come upon my premises.

The whole affair had escaped from my memory, and about an hour afterwards I was deeply immersed in some literary matters, when, from the day being close, and a revolver not the most comfortable thing to hang between one's chair and back, I removed mine from that position and laid it upon the table, where it soon became so smothered up among the various sheets of fools-cap, that a person unaware of the circumstance would scarcely have imagined that anything so dangerous lay in such close proximity to him.

While occasionally chatting with my landlord, or applying myself to my work, I was interrupted by the entrance into the room of Harris, in whose every lineament was expressed a determination to make himself disagreeable. Without an invitation he took a seat, made a few common-place remarks to my companion, and then, turning round sharply, demanded from me an explanation of the insult I had placed upon his children by calling them thieves, and forbidding them to come upon my premises. Fortunately I was so seated that I faced Harris, and, but for the table intervening between us, a collision would doubtless have occurred. I restrained my temper, however, only informing him that I had taken no steps without proper consideration, and that I was determined to enforce my resolution.

My antagonist, while pretending to listen to my remarks, drew from his bosom a bowie-knife, such as is generally used by hunters to skin deer. This formidable instrument he opened with pretended coolness, looking me full in the face with eyes that expressed a determination to make me intimate with its temper and quality. Shoving back the papers I picked up my pistol, and looking him full in the face, told him that I would regard one hostile movement on his part as a signal to fire. We stood thus for five minutes, the advantage which I had of possessing fire-arms alone saving me from being stabbed, possibly killed.

In the meantime my friend had not been idle, for he had taken from the gun-rack a double-barrel which was kept there constantly loaded, and thus armed threatened, by all that was high and low, to open fire on whomsoever commenced hostilities. What a tableau for the termination of a sensation drama! At length Harris, at being disappointed in his thirst for revenge, and muttering a volley of the foulest oaths, wheeled to the right about and departed, threatening vengeance on me at no very distant date. The better to guard myself against any future surprise by him, I told him, as he traversed the intermediate space between the house and the wicket-gate, that any trespass on his part over my private boundary would henceforth be regarded as an act of hostility.

It would be useless for me to deny that such a *contretemps* as had just occurred made me nervous, for it was evident that I had escaped by the nearest possible shave a hand-to-hand encounter with a desperate and reckless man. I knew, moreover, how much I was in his power, for almost any day, whether hunting in the woods or roaming over the prairie, he could give me the contents of his rifle at such range as would utterly incapacitate me from retaliating.

Soon after my landlord went out, depositing in the corner my gun, which he had lately taken possession of. Both for purposes of offence, or to have it ready at a moment's notice, if large game should suddenly make their appearance in the vicinity of the house, it contained good-sized shot in the right barrel, and heavy buck shot in the left.

Possibly half-an-hour might have elapsed when my friend returned; his face indicated that he was much excited. Taking a seat opposite me, he said, in a slow and measured voice, " Captain, I have bad news to communicate; I have just left Harris's house; he is, at this moment, moulding bullets, with which he vows to take your life before the sun goes down. I have argued and pleaded with him, but all that I can say is useless. The more I have urged the madness, on his part, of such a course, the more confirmed does he become in his diabolical resolution, and from my knowledge of his character, I feel certain as I am here that he will attempt what he says before the sun sets. I have ordered my horse to be saddled, and shall start at once for Judge ———, and obtain the assistance of the civil power to have this intended assassin placed in restraint till sufficient time has elapsed for his fit of evil temper to pass away. During my absence, let me beg of you not to leave the house, or expose yourself even at the windows."

In a few moments the sharp patter of horses' hoofs told that my landlord was *en route* at a rapid pace for the town. Possibly half-an-hour had elapsed, when hearing the creek which indicated that some person was opening the wicket gate, I looked through the window toward it, and there was Harris armed with his rifle, and the different paraphernalia he usually wore when hunting! Picking up my double-barrel, without the loss of a moment, I sprung to the door and sung out to him, in as plain language as I could use, that if he attempted to bring his rifle to his shoulder, I would shoot him where he stood. All persons acquainted with fire-arms are aware, that an ordinary gun, made for field-sports, has immense advantage in quickness of handling over the unwieldy long-barrelled American rifle, and that a charge or buck-shot at short range, if delivered with precision, must have a most destructive and fatal result. Thus fortune had again favoured me, and I was a second time master of the situation.

For some minutes my foe appeared undecided how to act, though he did not alter his position an inch. He, doubtless, observed resolution so plainly expressed in my manner, that he felt convinced I would fulfil to the letter the determination I had expressed. At the time he carried his rifle at the trail, in his left hand, and to employ it successfully it was necessary for him to pass his right across his chest, to grasp it so as to be able to bring it to the shoulder to take aim. Though the delay caused by this movement would be only momentary, still it would afford me sufficient time to kill any antagonist. Without further words we both eyed each other; hatred and a thirst for revenge on one side being apparent, while a fixed determination to put in execution a resolve deli-.berately formed was equally manifest on the other.

At length my enemy turned on his heel, and muttering his determination yet to do the deed he had contemplated, departed for his residence, while I heaved a sigh of relief that I had not been called upon to shed human blood even in self-defence.

CHAPTER VII.

WHEN Spring is rapidly approaching Summer,
oppressively warm days frequently occur that
produce in the human body a great disinclination
to exercise. I had resolved to have a final day
at the snipe, which were still numerous on the
prairie, and from the abundance of food, and
the warmth of the atmosphere, were so tame
that it required but little labour to procure a
heavy bag. This little labour, however, I did
not feel equal to, and therefore determined to

postpone my sport with the long-bills, *sine die.*

As I sat in my verandah and smoked and read, the broad and beautiful Wabash glittered in all the beauty of repose at my feet. Its cool waters looked so seductive, and its murmuring voice spoke so invitingly, that I determined to go down and have a swim. My shooting pony being as fond of a bath as myself, I went to the stable, placed on his head a snaffle, and bare-backed reached the margin of the river. In a few moments I was disrobed, and not without a certain amount of resemblance to a circus-rider, entered the stream on horseback. Up and down, backward and forward we paddled, each enjoying himself to the utmost.

I had only gained the margin sufficiently long to have donned those portions of male apparel which are put on first, when I observed a weather-beaten, sun-burnt, thick-bearded man toiling slowly along the road and evidently suffering from fatigue and galled feet. Though his costume had unquestionably seen service, it was clean and untorn, and had that unmistakable cut which indicates that its wearer had followed the sea. Although I and the pony were within twenty yards of the road, he tramped onward past us, evidently deeply absorbed in his own thoughts, which, judging from his expression, were none of the pleasantest.

At length the wayfarer halted, and sat down upon a log, the principal part of which was hid by a dense growth of sumach. Having put on all my apparel I mounted, and as I had to pass the stranger in my route to the house, I felt desirous to gratify my curiosity, and ascertain how a sailor had wandered so far from salt water. When I got opposite to the unknown, he raised his eyes till they caught mine, and rising to his feet, asked me how I thought he could get most speedily to Cleveland, Detroit, or any town upon the great Lakes.

" By railroad," I responded, " to Terre Haute."

" But," he continued, " if I walk it ? for I have no money."

"As you are going. This road follows the State line; but the distance is over two hundred miles," I added.

"That I know," he resumed; "but it is the nearest place where I can expect employment. I am a sailor, and here there is no use for persons of my trade."

He looked so sad, so tired, so hungry, and withal so manly, that my heart warmed to him, and dismounting, I seated myself at his side. In his voice, and manner of expressing himself, I soon detected that he was not an American, and without thinking that such a query might be construed into inquisitiveness, I asked him of what nation he was. He answered, unhesitatingly, that he came from England. Now whether he had been Turk or Nigger, if in distress or hungry I should have assisted him, but when I learned that he was from my own land, my heart warmed towards him, and I tendered food and a night's rest, at the same time asking him to accompany me. He did so, without reply, and I thanked Providence that I had been enabled to do a kind action.

Ere my house was reached, the man voluntarily told me some particulars of his past life. He had joined the gun-boat service of the United

States, and after saving money he had lost all by an accident. He had then been seized with fever and ague on the Lower Mississippi, and ultimately had been compelled to resign from utter incapacity, adding that he had never been strong since he was laid up with dysentery at Hong Kong.

"And when might that have been?" I asked, for I knew China well, had also suffered there from the same disease, and had only left the Celestial empire a few years back.

"At the termination of the last war," was his response; "I was on board the 'Feroze' with Lord Elgin, was at the taking of the Taku forts, and went up to Pekin afterwards."

Now here was a strange coincidence, to meet by chance in America one of the ten thousand men who had been my companions in that affair, we being at least ten thousand miles from the place where it had taken place.

I do not think that I actually required such a person about me; but I persuaded myself that

I did, and discovered lots of jobs peculiarly fitted to his talents, jobs which, previously, any person had performed; for I liked the man, and was pleased to talk of the past with him. Our conversations generally ended by the statement of our belief that England was the greatest and best country under the sun, and that Englishmen were the bravest, most generous, and most hospitable people on the face of the earth. To the sojourners in foreign lands England always appears a perfect garden of Eden.

There is one thing I am particularly partial to, and that is a nice garden. Flowers of every description I have the greatest love for, and vegetables I admire not only in the different stages of their growth, but as delicacies on the table, they are with me a weakness. After taking up my residence here I had the garden put in order. As soon as the frosts and snows had disappeared I devoted both time and money to the furtherance of my hobby, and had now the promise of such splendid crops that I felt more than recompensed for whatever outlay I had incurred. But the old adage, *L'homme propose, mais Dieu dispose,* has been verified in such a manner as to cause me much annoyance.

The garden, which is situated about fifty yards to the south of the house, contains about an acre of land. It is fenced externally with strong "posts-and-rails," backed on the inner side by a hedge of osage orange shrub. On the east side, this enclosure is bounded by a pasture field, generally appropriated to the use of the milch cows. Through some *intentional* mistake by my friend Harris, the work-oxen, eight or ten in number, were turned into this field last night, and the pasture in it being far from luxuriant, the confounded brutes sniffed the pleasant perfume emanating from my beans, peas, Spring cabbages, &c., and committed great ravages among them. One of the steers, familiarly known by the name of "Old Ball," was a notoriously bad character, the prime mover in all the mischief that his horned companions got into, and was so sly that he seldom was detected in time to prevent the successful accomplishment of any misdeeds that he intended to perpetrate.

When the sun was setting I took a stroll round the house and grounds, a habit I usually adopted, to see that all was secure upon my premises. Under a huge butternut tree, some way from the house, stood the patient oxen chewing their cuds, evidently at peace with all the world, and apparently with no thought of trespassing beyond their bounds. Satisfied with their appearance of harmlessness and assured of the strength of my fences, I retired to enjoy the hours that intervened between sunset and bedtime, for I had not yet been able to adopt the habit of going to rest with the termination of daylight.

Possibly I might have been an hour or two in bed, when I was awakened by the terriers making as great a disturbance as their shrill voices were capable of. Taking my revolver from under my pillow I sallied forth. The night was inky dark, and all my efforts to discover the cause of their uneasiness were therefore unavailing. Not for a moment imagining the true cause of their alarm, I turned into bed again, consoling myself with the idea that a fox, racoon, or opossum was prowling about the farm-yard in the expectation that a stray fowl might be picked up.

In the morning, however, I learned with sorrow the loss I had suffered, for the whole of the garden-fence on the field side had been levelled with the ground, and not a particle of vegetable left that the raiders could consume. The desolation was perfect, for even some toma-toes, choice tobacco plants, and cucumber vines, which had been rejected as unsuitable to their palates, were trampled down or torn up so as to prevent the slightest hope of their ever bear-ing fruit. The immense strength that an ox is possessed of is generally underrated, for no person would have thought it possible that a fence like the one that bounded this garden could have been demolished so thoroughly and with such apparent ease. Alas! thus in a few short hours were all my hopes of green peas, green corn, and other delicacies scattered to the winds.

In riding round the country, more particularly in those neighbourhoods where the population is sparse, and the soil has only lately been cultivated. I am surprised to observe the great number of persons who appear in the last stages of consumption. My first impression was that these invalids were suffering from the results of protracted fever and ague, which had so undermined their constitutions that the spirit was left without energy, and the body without power. In fact I was thoroughly depressed, feeling convinced that it could only be a matter of a week or two when, like the extinction of the flame of the candle that has burnt into the socket, life would pass from them.

On inquiring, however, I discovered that my conclusions were quite erroneous, the sufferings of these people proceeding neither from fever nor ague, but from a disease unknown in England, and as far as I can discover peculiar to America, where it is known far and wide as the " milk-sickness." Its germs are first sown in the human frame by either drinking the milk or eating the flesh of an animal that has become affected. The disease is so insidious and slow in its progress, on its first appearance in cattle, that for months they may have been inoculated with the virus before any perceptible change takes place in their appearance. A family may consequently be daily consuming milk or eating flesh, every portion of which is full of poison. Men, cows, and oxen are affected in the same manner by it. Their eyes protrude and become glazed, their strength gradually diminishes, and the body day by day becomes more emaciated. In some districts this ailment is so common that cattle produced in them are almost unsaleable, while milk, butter, and cheese, known to be made on farms within the dangerous bounds, cannot be sold at any price.

From authority that I have no reason to doubt, I have obtained information that there are immense tracts of the richest land lying on the lower waters of the Wabash that are entirely destitute of inhabitants, as no settler can remain there without himself and family becoming victims to this scourge. The State Legislature have offered a reward of twenty thousand dollars to any person who may discover the cause of this disease. The promise of such a sum of money, as may naturally be expected, drew scientific men from far and near; but all their inquiries and researches were in vain, and its origin is, at the present moment, wrapt up in as much mystery as when its existence was first discovered.

Out of more than a dozen theories as to what produces the milk-sickness, I will state three, each of which has numerous advocates. The first is, that the cattle are bitten by snakes; secondly, that they eat some noxious herbage, and lastly, that by licking a species of shale which is exceedingly saline in taste, they take into their systems a mineral poison. On one point all unite, that Summer is the season when the mischief commences, and from this I should incline to the opinion of those who attribute it to an unknown herb, as at that season, from the heat of the sun, and the torment all cattle suffer from under the constant persecution of flies, they retire from the open ground to the grateful shade afforded by the woods.

Before leaving a subject which, if only from a desire to benefit those who suffer from such a scourge to their stock, deserves much attention, I would add that, like others, I have had my surmises as to what produces the disease. When in South Africa, I heard many of the residents, particularly those that travel in the interior, speak of the " tsetse " fly, which is so destructive to domestic cattle that, when a region known to abound with them is traversed by traders, the journeys are made at night to avoid the persecution of these destructive insects; but when an ox is bitten by them, loss of appetite and decrease of flesh—symptoms, in fact, similar to those arising from milk-sickness—are exhibited. In the bottom lands of the Wabash may there not exist, not exactly a tsetse fly, but an insect similarly noxious?

I had not discovered the existence of this malady before, because every resident avoids conversation on this point in the presence of strangers; for all new arrivals are looked on as future citizens, or immediate purchasers of land

and cattle, and as " every little makes a mickle," the addition of even one person to the existing number of inhabitants adds to the value of property.

The payment of the purchase-money of a landed estate may, moreover, put a citizen in possession of sufficient hard cash to transport his *lares et penates* to more favoured regions, while he allows the ignorant stranger to settle in a spot which assuredly he would not have selected if he had been informed that milk-sickness was known to exist upon it, or even within miles of it.

At one period this locality perfectly abounded with rattlesnakes, but now they are comparatively scarce. Their destruction was principally accomplished by the introduction of hogs, which greedily feed upon these reptiles whenever chance throws them in their way. I have several times had opportunities of watching a pig engaged in an encounter with one of these snakes, which they worry, as a clever terrier would a rat. The hog attacks the rattlesnake with such energy and rapidity that the assailed reptile has scarcely time to guard himself against the attack, when he finds himself in the fatal grasp of his too powerful foe.

The copper-head snake was also at one time very numerous in Southern Indiana and Illinois, but it likewise has much decreased in number, although not to the same extent as the former reptile. In appearance it is short in proportion to its length, but has a very large head. It varies from dark brown to black along the vertebræ, gradually changing to a dull copper tint along the stomach.

These creatures are exceedingly venomous; but I believe they will not attack any animal unless molested. The name " Copperhead " has been applied lately by the Federals to all persons of Southern sympathies, more especially to those who still remain north of Mason and Dixon's line.

My bed-room windows open down almost to the ground. Around them are trained some *pyrus japonica* and Virginian ivy. On entering my room one morning after breakfast, I observed to my surprise the head and shoulders of a snake protruding over the sill, cautiously taking a survey of the interior of the apartment. To make certain of accomplishing the destruction of the would-be intruder, I quietly retired, and having obtained my double gun, went out by the back-door, and made a *détour* round the house till I came to a position whence I could observe him. Alarmed at my presence, the snake made a most precipitate retreat towards the porch of the hall door, but a charge of shot put him *hors de combat* ere shelter could be reached.

On examination, I found I had killed a very large specimen of the American puff-adder, out of whose stomach I exhumed a chicken quite three weeks old. I was more than pleased at this circumstance, for the disappearance of all the young fowl from the poultry-yard was generally attributed to the malpractices of my setters.

Armed with the unfortunate fledgling, I proceeded to Mrs. Kelly, keeper of the fowls, to demonstrate, by the convincing proof I held in my hand, that Beau at least was not guilty of all the misappropriations of chickens that took place; but it is not an easy task to convince a woman against her will, and so deaf was she to all my arguments that I do not believe I succeeded in convincing her that my favourites had been unjustly calumniated. Give a dog a bad name and you may hang him. My dog had really got a very bad name, and I confidently believe without sufficient reason; but as to hanging him, why, money would not have parted us.

I have learned that for years a family of puff-adders have resided under the large stone that forms the flooring of the porch to the hall door, that every attempt to dislodge them has failed, and that one of the farm-servants had suffered a long and painful illness from the bite of one of these unwelcome tenants. The specimen I had deprived of life was doubtless one of this family circle, which I hoped yet to become still more intimate with.

By the advice of my temporary cook, a cross
between an Indian and a nigger, who, from
his intimate knowledge of the habits of animals
was reputed to be skilled in all matters connected with the chase, I left the body of the
adder close to the hole by which they entered
their retreat, and placed myself in a position
that enabled me to fire upon any of the
reptiles coming out to inspect the dead
one.

I watched in vain for half an hour, and when
at length dinner was announced I left my position of observation, determining to return as
soon as the meal was over. On revisiting my
post, I had the good fortune to obtain a view
of what I supposed to be the partner of the
defunct, and had the satisfaction of putting an
end to his earthly career. My work of an-
nihilation, however, was only partially performed, for several youngsters still survived their
parents.

I had long looked forward to a visit from a
very old friend who lives more than a hundred
miles to the north-east of my residence, but he

had so often deprived me of the promised pleasure of making me his host, that I had at last
unwillingly resigned myself to the conviction
that I should never see him as my guest. It
is many years now since we met, and during
our intercourse we had gone through so many
exciting scenes together, that I had looked forward
with some degree of certainty to the pleasure of
conversing with him on old events and old
friends.

It is always interesting to recall the escapades
of youth in the society of one who has par-
ticipated in them. The ideas, the thoughts, the
feelings of former days return to the mind, and
the passage of time is so far forgotten that one
imagines he is for the moment living over again
the period so long past.

In searching over numerous scraps written to
commemorate past events, I find that I possess
a narrative of our first and only meeting, and
although the scene of it is far from my present
residence, I give it to show how small this world
is to those who have travelled much; for there is

no nook or corner of it where you can so completely hide your head that former friends
and associates will not succeed in finding you
out.

CHAPTER VIII.

Sailing along the Coast of Algeria—An American in Valetta—
A Storm in the Mediterranean—French Troops in Bona—
An English Zouave—On Horseback—A dog *pour la Chasse*
—A Charming Vivandière—A Stern Chase—A Confession of
Love—Shooting Quarters

THERE are few things more agreeable than
sailing along the coast of Algeria in fine weather,
with the wind off shore. The sea is generally so
calm and blue, the shore so bold and grand,
and the distant high grounds are so soft in
shade and picturesque in outline, that all form
a picture of what fairy-land might be. Is it to
be wondered, then, that, having enjoyed a trip
through this portion of the Mediterranean under
the most favourable auspices, I should have
desired to repeat it, more particularly as I

M 2

learned from a French officer of Spahis that
Algeria was the perfection of a sporting
country?

The drill season was nearly finished, and what
between brigade days, scaling drill, and com-
manding officer's inspection, all under the
rank of field-officers were commencing to feel
surfeited with their unceasing repetition. The
Winter, moreover, had not been so enjoyable as
usual, the Governor unfortunately being what is
frequently denominated "not one of the right
stamp;" and as human beings are very much like
a flock of sheep in following the example of their
leaders, balls, parties, and convivialities were
far from numerous.

Our Colonel, too, was a morose old growler,
who believed in perfect rank and file and perfect
officers, regarding both as machines. His
orderly-room duties were long and tedious, his
inspection of kits and accounts of unneces-
sarily frequent occurrence, and mufti was
tabooed by the most rigorous interdictions.
Such stern decorum reigned in the ante-room
after dinner that conversation was chiefly

carried on in monosyllables. Is it then astonish-
ing that I should have hailed with delight a
favourable response to my application for a
month's leave of absence?

Among the strangers who had visited Valetta
was an American whom I stumbled across
one evening at the circulating library in Strada
Reale. The pretty wife of the proprietor of the
establishment introduced us, and we soon became
on most friendly terms. He had left home to
see the world and enjoy himself, and being
possessed of abundant means had every opportunity of doing so. This gentleman agreed to
accompany me in my trip to Algeria.

Journeys by water are so much alike that
it is unnecessary to enter into many details of our voyage to the coast of Africa.
Suffice it to say that before we embarked we
endured with stoicism the importunities of
the beggars—the attempt at pilfering of the
boatmen who took us on board the craft on
which we had taken passage—the stamping and
swearing of captain and sailors—and, though last
not least, the pervading odours of garlic and

oil. The Fates seemed to favour us at starting, for the wind blew aft, and soon St. Elmo's light faded into indistinctness—Gozzo soon after following suit, while Pantaleria, like an immense triangle suspended in the air, loomed upon our port bow.

The changeable weather in this locality invariably reminded me of the temper of its inhabitants. The balmy six-knot breeze which a few hours previously had been blowing was now something like a gale, and our boat close-hauled was pitching into a heavy head sea; the white crested waves which surrounded us in all directions holding high carnival.

Hour after hour the gale increased, becoming so violent that we could scarcely carry more canvas than would have made a moderate-sized pocket-handkerchief. The gasconading and blustering of the crew diminished in an equal ratio with the growing violence of the elements, so that, when their services were most desirable for the proper handling of our storm-tossed barque, they lay stowed away in such corners as afforded most shelter, counting their beads and vowing

to live for the future the most irreproachable
lives, if Providence would only permit them to
place their feet again upon *terra firma*. Either
these supplications were heard, or we were
reserved for future and greater trials, for we
weathered our way through the storm, our craft
jumping over or bobbing her nose into the seas,
as she strained, creaked, and worked through
many tedious hours, till, before the setting of
the sun on the second day, the gale blew
itself out, and with a gentle and favourable
breeze we dropped anchor in the port of our destination.

No nation on the face of the earth so
thoroughly enjoy soldiering as the French, and
this was then seen in Algeria; for a distant tribe
had declared war to the knife against the inva-
ders of their soil. The serious manner with
which *La Grande Nation* treat the most minute
details of service, is, to an Englishman, ludicrous;
and their worship of medals, ornaments, gold
lace, &c., amounts, in the eyes of a phlegmatic
Briton, to absurdity. In Bona all was bustle
and confusion; troops were daily arriving

and departing; ambulance waggons blocked the streets, aide-de-camps and orderlies galloped to and fro, Zouaves mustered in cliques around the canteens, and, light in heart and careless in manner, laughed, joked, and expressed themselves in animated pantomimic action; while grave field, staff, or general officers, invariably with cigars in their mouths, looked as if the fate, not of France only, but of the world, lay on their shoulders.

A letter of introduction with which my friend was armed procured us accommodation which otherwise we should have had difficulty in obtaining, for every nook and cranny was filled with troops or camp-followers. Although the apartment allotted to our use was anything but such as we should have selected from choice, we put up, considering the circumstances, with limited accommodation and incessant flea-bites without a complaint.

Our arrival was soon known. Visitors poured in rapidly, and the courtesies showered upon us were too numerous to mention. During our short sojourn we supped, dined, or breakfasted with one or other of our new friends; and the *bonne camaraderie* resulting from a common profession and our late alliance in the Crimea confuted all those antiquated ideas that Frenchmen are born enemies to the inhabitants of Great Britain.

Frenchmen, however, are not sportsmen in our acceptation of the word. The information I obtained was, to my disappointment and disgust, so contradictory that I feared we had made a great blunder in our selection of localities, and would have to return without pulling a trigger.

While in this irresolute state, a visitor knocked at our door. The sound startled me, for it was exactly that of a London postman. On being told to enter, in walked a Zouave, rank " full private." With a little apparent hesitation he informed me, in the most perfect English, that he was a countryman, and had taken the liberty of calling, as he was anxious to know if the 48th Regiment were in Malta, and, if so, whether I would take a letter back with me for his brother, a non-commissioned officer in that corps.

It did not appear rude to be inquisitive regarding the affairs of a stranger of so humble
a grade, and between countrymen, when they
meet abroad, out of the usual track of travel,
there is a species of free-masonry; so, in
answer to my inquiries, I learned that my
visitor had been a postman in our metro-
polis.

As there are very few Englishmen that have
not a liking for field-sports, it struck me that
this man might possibly know something of the
capabilities of the country in this respect; and as
luck would have it, we obtained from him lucid
information as to the game to be found in different localities—all of which bore the ring of true
metal.

The next morning, ere the sun had shown
over the eastern high grounds, we were *en
route*, mounted on borrowed horses. Our
appearance drew much attention, and we were
objects of great curiosity to military and to civi-
lians alike. This appeared surprising with reference to myself, for in costume and equipment
I believed myself so perfect that I might have

been seen by any cover in our Midland counties during Autumn. I prided myself, moreover, on my horsemanship, a fair friend having once whispered in my ear that I never looked to such advantage as in the pigskin.

My friend, however, most certainly could never have been on horseback before, for his attention seemed to be so entirely absorbed in endeavouring to retain his equilibrium that he was unable, for the time, to exert his conversational powers. His nag, being fresh and restive, showed a decided objection to the gun in the hands of its rider, and though for an hour the representative of the great Western Republic stuck like a man to his double-barrel, he was at last so worried and chafed that he consented to its being carried by one of the ambulance drivers proceeding in our direction.

I must not forget to mention that we had two dogs. Mine was an orthodox old pointer that might have passed muster in any crowd. The other one, borrowed by my

friend, had been represented · as a splendid dog *pour la chasse,* but his appearance
was so peculiar that it would have puzzled
the most skilled in the canine science to
pronounce what crosses or breeds had combined to produce him. I had protested against
this addition to our party, but, being over-
ruled, " Cæsar " became one of us. The *genus
canis,* like the *genus homo* has its peculiarities; and one of Master Cæsar's was that
he had a thorough detestation of the half-
civilized specimens of his own race that were
to be met with along the highway. He was
so unwearied in giving them chase that I
almost imagined him impervious to fatigue;
for during the few leagues we had traversed,
he must have gone quadruple the distance
in pursuit of these wild four-footed brethren.

Towards noon we halted at a canteen where,
under the shade of an aloe hedge, we quaffed
sundry glasses of *vin ordinaire,* and entered into
most agreeable conversation with a party of
young officers, evidently just arrived from home

and thirsting after military glory. When our cigars were almost smoked out, a *vivandière* joined our group, a wild harum-scarum reckless piece of goods, with an answer for everybody, and exhibiting such proficiency at repartee that very few indeed could claim the victory in a contest of words with her. In appearance she was *petite* and well-formed, with the largest and most wicked oriental-looking eyes, while a wealth of glossy black hair fell unconfined from under her forage cap around her shoulders. With that courtesy to the fair sex so characteristic of Americans, my friend was at once most marked in his attentions to her. A mutual liking sprung up between them; and when we again got into the saddle, this light-hearted vivacious "daughter of the regiment" proposed to be of our party throughout the next stage.

It is an old saying that two are company, but three none. This adage was so pointedly recalled to my memory by the continual whisperings and *sub rosa* looks interchanged between my fellow-traveller and the sprightly

child of France, that to avoid being considered
a bore, and very much against my will—for I
too had a hankering for her society—I acceler-
ated the pace of my nag so as to get out of
ear-shot, and lead the way. While doing so
a cur sprung from under a bush, and if a kettle
had been attached to his tail he could not have
made a more precipitate flight. Cæsar marked
the game, and giving tongue like a fox-hound
started in pursuit. In pace he had the best of
it, and, but for an unexpected event his teeth
would doubtless, in a few more strides, have
become acquainted with the flanks of the fugitive.

The harassed brute, however, turning suddenly
round, seized Cæsar by the throat, and in less
time than words can describe threw him on his
back. Three or four other curs rushed at the
same time to the assault, with such vindictive
demonstrations, that it at once became evident that, but for prompt interference, our
grand sporting dog would be torn limb from
limb.

The *vivandière* and my friend evidently saw

things in the same light, and it became a race between us who should get first to the rescue. The lady won by a neck, but our arrival did not put a stop to the contest, so determined were the belligerents in their rage and fury. My heavy built, powerful old pointer, moreover, joined in the fight in defence of his acquaintance, thus adding fuel to the fire.

It is not safe or easy to interfere with seven or eight dogs in an indiscriminate heap, biting and tearing each other, as my friend evidently thought, for he endeavoured to intimidate the bellicose brutes by riding them down. The plan to a certain extent succeeded; but one of the curs, before taking his departure, laid hold of his horse by the hock. Bucephalus plunged, reared, and kicked. For a moment the rider gallantly retained a seat somewhere between the ears and tail; but all his efforts to ward off the calamity were unavailing, and he was finally dismounted—his appearance, in his descent, being not unlike that of a huge spread eagle taking a header.

In performing this acrobatic feat, he let go

his reins, and the horse, released from captivity,
immediately took to flight. I saw at a glance
the inconvenience that must result from the loss
of the animal's services. Mlle. Vivandière was
evidently struck with the same idea, though she
continued 'to give way to the most abundant
merriment at my friend's disaster.

We both, however, started in pursuit of the
truant, and never was there a more interesting
race. The little merry elf was determined to beat
me, and the few straggling soldiers who were
around apparently believed I was unable to
obtain the lead. Such a thought had not
entered my head, but, if it had, her light
weight and superior mount would have given her
so much advantage that I could only have
expected to come off second best.

A stern chase is always a long one, and
we had passed over a mile before the daring
little horsewoman was alongside the fugitive.
He would not, however, permit himself to be
captured, and possibly a mile and a half more
were traversed before we were able to lay hold
of the reins. I have ridden with fox-hounds,

harriers, and beagles, but never enjoyed a run with greater gusto than this one; for I had commenced with a partiality for the little woman, which certainly was damped when I saw her show such a decided leaning to my companion. As she galloped before me, each stride of her horse displayed new points of perfection in her figure.

When we had made our capture we both halted. Riders as well as horses required a respite, which it is scarcely necessary to say was not hurried. My friend's disaster had not elevated him in the opinion of the martial beauty, who, evidently considering want of skill in equitation a great fault in a man, chattered a whole vocabulary of chaff at the ridiculous figure he had cut and the trouble he had caused.

Ultimately satisfied that I was making rapid strides in her favour, I gained courage enough to manufacture an excuse for dismounting, by stating that the girths of my saddle had become slack. After going through a semblance of taking up a hole or two, I found what I considered a favourable opportunity, and endeavoured to kiss the little one's hand. In return I received a box on the ear, no light one I can assure you, while in the most *non-chalant* manner she exclaimed, " You Englishmen are so clumsy."

I felt snubbed of course, but determined not to show it, so we chatted on about all descriptions of irrelevant matters, till we found our unlucky friend still seated on the ground, apparently on the identical spot where he had kissed mother earth. His countenance looked woe-begone in the extreme, and when he gained his legs it was evident that his nether garments had suffered sadly in the disaster.

It is seldom a man can enter into a joke against himself, and my American friend certainly could not. From fear, therefore, of producing a quarrel, I was obliged to look serious; but the little dame did not. She chaffed the poor fellow to such an extent that it required no small amount of self-control to suppress my inclination to laughter.

On the second day, however, we parted from her, and it was not a moment too soon, for somehow or other we always found ourselves alone together.

Nowhere are there more beautiful moonlight nights than in Algeria, more particularly in the Spring of the year. Nightingales sing from every tree, goatsuckers glide by on noiseless wings, occasionally uttering their plaintive call; while the shrill voice of the jackal so frequently heard there, particularly if mellowed by distance, is far from being unpleasant. It was on such an evening, and while we were listening to such sounds, that we parted. I had strolled from the Arab house, where I intended sleeping, to finish my cigar. A little way off burnt a camp-fire, around which lounged a dozen soldiers, their martial figures in their brilliant uniforms standing out in bold relief against the surrounding gloom. I joined them, and was at once made welcome. Ten minutes afterwards I was sharply tapped on the shoulder. It was the *vivandière*.

"So Monsieur leaves us to-morrow! Is it

not so?" she commenced in a careless manner.

"Too true, I am sorry to say," I answered.

"Sorry did you say?" she repeated twice."

"Yes, sorry!"

"And why so?"

"It is better not to confess."

"Well, I am sorry also, and I will confess. Come!" She took my arm, and we slowly walked away from the fire.

For some minutes neither spoke. At length she halted, and, turning round while she looked me steadily in the face, said,

"I am sorry because I like you—almost love you. If you were a soldier of France I would retain my confession, because we should meet again somewhere or other, but when you go it is never to return. You will wander off to distant lands, and day after day will separate us further. You could not make me your wife, because"—and she here hesitated, but again continued with perceptible agitation. "If I had been one of our fashionable dames, artificial in figure and form, deceitful in tongue and mercenary at heart, it would have been different," and she stamped her foot.

I dared not answer. I was so astonished and pained. I had possibly flirted with her, but never dreamt that my attentions were greater than those she received daily from others. I held her hand in mine, and was about to say something to soothe her agitation, when she again spoke:

"All I ask is your likeness. You will not refuse my request. I will keep it, for it will represent the first man I have met that I could have loved."

I promised to send it from Malta, on my return.

"Remember you keep your word; it is on your honour you make it." And ere the echoes of the last words had died from my ears, she was gone.

Next day, at noon, we reached our shooting quarters. An Algerine we had sent forward had obtained, in a douar, possession of a hut for our accommodation, situated on the apex of some high land. This, having been well swept out, had the advantage of at least looking clean. The view around was exactly such as a sportsman might desire, for the country was open, rolling, and park-like,—the slopes being covered with dwarf palmetto or grass. Half a mile off, numerous giant oleanders marked a water course, and through their stems the crystal liquid could be seen at intervals. That evening, as the Moslem priest chanted forth his summons to call the faithful to worship, the sun set in refulgent glory behind the western hills, portending the continuance of fine weather.

As I stood and gazed with that interest which the wanderer always finds in new scenes, numerous cattle, sheep, and goats came trooping up the slope, under the protection of several stalwart herds, draped in their flowing white burnouses—evidence of a wealth not suggested by their primitive and roughly-constructed habitations. There was a freedom and simplicity, yet wildness, in the scene, most attractive to my mind.

Up to this time I had not paid any attention

to my friend's shooting gear. Before retiring
for the night, as we intended making an early
start, we proceeded to make our guns ready
for service, and I took an opportunity to examine
my companion's double-barrel, but of all the
trash I ever saw made up in the shape of a
gun—and my experience has been considerable—
this one beat them all by long odds. Who was
its maker must for ever remain a mystery, for
no person in his senses would have branded
himself with infamy by engraving his name on
such a combination of wood and iron. Ten
dollars at the utmost must have been its cost,
and he who gave such a sum for it verified the
proverb of the fool and his money. I actually
think a good shake would have parted the stock
and barrels.

Such a discovery, the evening before commencing operations, was far from agreeable.
True, I was not to shoot with the vile weapon, but
it might burst at my side, with equally bad
personal consequences; so I resolved at least to
give my friend a wide berth.

With 'baccy and a night-cap we betook ourselves to our ground sheet-beds, where we should have doubtless enjoyed an uninterrupted night of rest, but that Master Cæsar managed to steal out unobserved, just, I suppose, as we had got thoroughly into the arms of Morpheus, and soon made his absence known by engaging in a most determined encounter with all the dogs of the douar. Poor old Sancho, my favourite, heard the turmoil, and with stentorian lungs bewailed the arrangements which prevented him from proceeding to the rescue. As the borrowed dog could not be left to be devoured, without some attempt on our part to prevent such a catastrophe, we, with our attendant, sallied forth in our sleeping attire.

Each of us therefore picked up a stout club before leaving the house, but many vigorous blows were received before the struggling canine mass could be parted into its units. Cæsar, game to the last, was not rescued a moment too soon, for the blood flowed in numerous wounds from his yellow hide. As he proved such a constant source of annoyance, he was condemned to be kept constantly tied up for the future. I almost wished he had been hanged, for I was uncharitable enough to believe him quite incapable of performing his duties in the field.

My friend snored through the remaining hours of that night, while I kicked and tossed about most uncomfortably. But day at last dawned, and with the increasing light, cattle, horses, goats, sheep, and poultry indicated, by their various calls, their proximity; expressing at the same time their desire to be released from confinement. Semi-civilized people, subsisting as these dwellers in Northern Africa do, seldom require such summonses to leave their dormitories. Habit has become second nature to them, and as few are troubled with elaborate wardrobes, very little delay occurs between rising and going forth. Perhaps I should rather say that *our* habits have become second nature, those of these keepers of flocks being much more primitive and in accordance with the teachings of Nature.

CHAPTER IX.

Good Sport—Al-fresco Luncheon—Cæsar—Encounter with
a Panther—Boar at Bay—African Sport—Return to Bona.
—Bad Weather.

OUR advent in shooting was eminently propitious. Quail in single and double birds were
flushed from every bunch of palmettos. I shot
moderately, my friend badly. Still the capa-
cious game-bags which were suspended on either
side of a horse ridden by our guide commenced
to expand. From the higher hill-sides we
descended into a large expanse of wet meadow,
where snipe, plover, and wild duck were abundant, and from these we made a selection to add
to our miscellaneous spoil. We ate our lunch

by the side of a cool spring, under the shade of a giant fig-tree, and enjoyed our *otium* without any attempt at dignity. Cæsar was not of the party, having been left at home tied up, in consequence of the physical disqualifications for field services under which he suffered. His grief at being denied the privilege of accompanying us was vouched for by his doleful howlings, which gradually became less and less distinct as the distance increased between us and the village.

I considered the *contretemps* of last evening a very fortunate circumstance, for otherwise I should have had to submit to his eccentricities in running up game, and scouring the country giving tongue.

We were not yet out of the wood, however, for our frugal meal was barely finished when, to my consternation, the subject of my dislike put in an appearance (limping on three legs, and with about a couple of yards of rope trailing behind him), with the greatest manifestations of pleasure. His injuries had told upon him, for he was a sadder if not a wiser dog, and only gratified his propensity for mischief, by giving such wounded birds as fell in his way a vicious pinch.

After lunch we again made for the more elevated regions, and on a bank facing the south, covered with scrub, found several coveys of red-legged partridges not yet paired. After numerous shots we broke them up, many of them winging their way to a neighbouring hill-side, while the remainder turned back to the ground we had just traversed.

My friend whose name, by the by, was Smith—yes, John Smith, but no relation of the worthy that figures so prominently in American history, had come to the conclusion that his indifferent shooting was produced by the irregular action of the locks and general indifferent quality of his wondrous gun. He therefore asked, as a personal favour, that I would exchange arms with him for a few minutes, while he went back after the birds that had doubled round and dropped in our rear. To refuse such a request would have been simply ungentlemanly, and I handed him my weapon, while armed with his I started for the birds that had alighted on the neighbouring slope.

The attendant instructed to retain a higher position on the incline than I did, and endeavour to "mark" the birds on their future resting places, accompanied me; but on arrival at the ground, my game was nowhere to be found. I cast backwards and forwards, and gave Sancho the wind, but all without avail, though a quarter of an hour was thus consumed. The birds had doubtless taken flight, unperceived, while the negotiation for an exchange of guns was taking place.

While I was thinking of giving up the unproductive search, my attention was attracted to our guide, who was by turns gesticulating violently with his arms and pointing to a water-course beneath. I had no doubt that he saw some description of game in the direction indicated, and directed my steps towards it; but this proceeding was evidently not to his satisfaction, for his pantomimic gestures became more and more numerous and grotesque.

I could see water from where I stood, among

the oleander limbs, and some animal was apparently disturbing its surface. This rivulet had not an uninterrupted course, but was broken into pools, the connecting links between which were hidden among the gigantic boulders that studded its course. The current consequently was barely perceptible, and water only visible at those places where the bottom was extremely low.

Disregarding my guide, I descended quietly, feeling confident I was about to have a shot at wild duck. To improve my prospect of success, and shorten the range, I made a detour so as to come out on the reverse side of the pool, which, to all appearance, was much more free from cover.

With bent back and cautious, slow, and measured step, I advanced upon the supposed broad-bills, not a quack or flutter indicating their presence, till I was certainly well within shot. The last bunch of oleander that intercepted my view was pushed on one side, and I stood in the presence—not of a clique of the web-footed family—but within eight or at the furthest ten yards—of an enormous panther!

In previous years, in America, I had killed dangerous game, but on all occasions, except one, with suitable arms. The exception alluded to was on one occasion when I came upon a bear at the closest possible range, and then duck-shot was in my barrels instead of No. 7, which I now possessed. I may admit I felt alarmed, but the rencontre had the effect of so bracing me that I prepared coolly for any overt action on the part of the enemy.

Our discovery of each other's presence occurred simultaneously. The panther slowly raised its head from the water in which it had been drinking, but its body remained extended at full length, the twitching of its tail and the almost imperceptible gathering back of the ears being the sole indications of animation. The eyes, however, those wonderful indexes of character, or rather intention, in a beast of prey, spoke, as plainly as any language could, the anger with which my intrusion was regarded. It was useless to sigh after impossibilities, but what would I not have given to have my own trusty double gun, each barrel loaded with ball, when I might have taken the initiative and not felt disposed to sneak away from so worthy an antagonist.

The knowledge I had acquired from the study of wild animals alone saved me. I stood prepared for the worst, staring straight into the face of my adversary, determined only to use my gun at close quarters. My cool demeanour and determined aspect would, however, I hoped, induce the brute to avoid provoking a conflict. My steady stare and bold gaze had the desired effect, for, after the lapse of a few minutes, the animal arose, took a parting look at me, and then, turning slowly, disappeared almost as silently as a shadow.

The moral victory I well knew was mine, and no longer satisfied with being safe from so dangerous a foe, I emerged from the bushes to see the game steal across the open which it was necessary to traverse ere it could reach cover of sufficient magnitude to shelter it perfectly from view. I was not a moment too soon, for the panther was within thirty or forty yards of the cover, and a few more bounds would transport it out of sight, when confound it! there was that extraordinary dog Cæsar close at its heels and gaining on the object of his pursuit at every stride, while a short distance to my right was Smith hurrying towards me as rapidly as the rough surface of the ground would permit.

It was now apparent to what I owed my safety. The noise caused by the advance of my friend had been heard by the panther, and not relishing the prospect of a double duel it had preferred flight. Meanwhile the rash Cæsar was almost within such distance of the panther as would enable him to use his teeth, and the energy which characterised his bearing spoke his purpose; but he had a crafty and powerful foe to deal with.

In a moment the panther turned, and without an apparent effort struck a blow which elicited from Cæsar a short deep howl of pain. The poor animal, wounded unto death, lay struggling on the ground, the wild cat disappearing a moment afterwards into the brush.

How far the formidable creature would go when out of sight was doubtful, for stealthy and cunning as all its race, it might now be only a few yards off from its struggling victim, and it was therefore necessary to be more than usually careful in approaching the dog.

This I pointed out to my companion; but his blood was up, and in spite of consequences the plucky dog must be attended to. Our attendant, who now joined us, told us he had seen the panther crossing at a rapid pace some bare ground a hundred yards or more from the place where it had taken cover.

Poor Cæsar was truly in a pitiable condition. His back was broken, and several deep gashes scored his flank. Yet although it was apparent that he was suffering intense agony, which could terminate only in death, the poor fellow looked into his temporary master's eyes with an air which seemed to express the satisfaction he felt at having done his duty like a good dog, and licked the hand extended to caress him.

Nothing could be done for the sufferer, and I proposed, as an act of charity, to terminate his sufferings, but a stern interjection of dissent was the response. Such a step, however, was not necessary, for, with a painful whine the poor creature made an effort to stretch itself, and after a few spasmodic struggles all was over.

A fixed purpose of revenge was evidently paramount in the bosom of my companion. It is useless to describe· the nights, fruitless of results, that he passed stationed on lonely hillsides, or in rocky ravines, provided with a kid as bait to tempt the object of his search within range of his barrels, but at length repeated want of success damped his ardour, and our time was again devoted to small game.

We had returned from shooting one day a little earlier than usual. In the douar was a horseman—a splendid specimen of his race. To us was intended the honour of his visit. He told us that " at a hamlet ten miles off wild hogs were causing serious destruction to the crops, and would the Feringees pass a few days with the sheik, and assist to kill some of the noxious animals?" As change of scene was beginning to to be desirable, the invitation was promptly accepted.

Our ride next morning, after the first few miles, was through what was to us a new country. Dense copses of exaggerated brush were of frequent occurrence, while a lagoon of considerable extent, and well stocked with aquatic game, stretched for some miles to the left. Whenever our path led over the damp ground, soil turned up, with water resting in the indentations, told of the nocturnal visits of master piggy to the locality. The village reached, we held a levee in the hut allotted for our reception, when, through the medium of our guide, our course of proceeding for the morrow was settled.

When, at length, with the exception of the sheik and our visitor of yesterday, we were alone, coffee, seasoned with something stronger, and tobacco were in great demand; and the two

Christian dogs, particularly when they succeeded in making it understood that they were not French, made rapid strides in the estimation of their host. In a position such as this, it is impossible to over-estimate the disadvantage of not speaking the language of the inhabitants. Interpreters never do justice to either party, often abbreviating your most flowery speeches and compliments, and that, doubtless, in a most ruthless way.

In spite, however, of these little difficulties, the *entente cordiale* was so thoroughly established that ere it was dark we had all started together for some neighbouring gardens, with the hope of getting a shot at an immense boar which nightly ravaged them.

The sheik and the American took up their position in some tall dry reeds, beside an enclosure of grain, as yet only a few inches above the surface of the soil, while my companion and myself pushed forward nearly half a mile further to a tangled thicket of scrub which flanked what evidently had been a sweet potato and melon ground. The wind suited

the position of our ambush, and it was soon
made as comfortable as circumstances would
permit.

If it is tedious to lie on a sick-bed
anxiously waiting the return of day, it is still
more trying to one's patience to be caged in
a bush, unable to move, even to yawn, for
fear of alarming your quarry; while at the
same time you are debarred the comfort of
tobacco, lest its fumes should taint the atmosphere, for the wild animals invariably associate
man with the Nicotian leaf.

But it was a beautiful night. Although not
so clear as day, there was sufficient light to
see distinctly objects within thirty or more
yards—that subdued light that softens the
outline, and gives additional attraction to all
you gaze on.

Several false alarms had been given. A
rustling bough or broken twig had recalled
me from some reflections in which I was indulging, to the realities of my position. Still
nothing appeared, and no report of fire-arms
indicated that my friend had been vouched

greater luck. In a few moments, however, the Arab laid his hand upon my wrist, a muffled sound, not distant, but subdued, having struck upon his ear. I heard it too, and my heart palpitated with eager excitement. The noise continued, and after the lapse of a short time it became more and more apparent that it heralded the approach of some animal.

The eye is wonderfully apt to exaggerate. For this reason, probably, sportsmen often get the credit of not adhering closely to the truth; but it is a positive fact that, as soon as I could distinguish the figure of my quarry, I thought it was at least as large as a donkey. It was advancing directly towards me, its head bent down in the act apparently of examining the surface in search of favourite roots. In uncertain light I am not partial to end shots, for they require much precision, and I therefore waited for a broadside. Although the animal was within twenty yards of me, no such opportunity offered for some minutes, but it came at last. A twig that had been doubled under our seat escaped from the pressure and with a slight noise abruptly straightened itself.

This alarmed the animal, which, with a short energetic grunt threw its head up, and turned round on its guard. My barrels were pointed in a moment to his shoulder, which was exposed, and simultaneously with the report piggy fell.

Springing to my feet, I threw down my butt to load, for this was in the days of muzzle-loaders, and down went the wad over the powder. The creature which I supposed to be dying struggled violently in the spasmodic efforts, as I believed, that precede death. In this, however, I was mistaken, for on a sudden it gained its feet, and before I could throw in a second shot the stricken game had vanished into the gloom.

On our way home we thought to find our friends, but they were gone. On our arrival at the village we learned that they had not yet returned. So, tired, and possibly disgusted at my want of luck, I retired to my couch, grateful for the possession of such a luxury, although consisting only of a few blankets and a ground-sheet.

An hour after midnight Smith came home. He had obtained three shots, the result of which was bagging one hog, wounding a second, and missing the third. My tale, as unvarnished as possible, was then told; after which, it was settled that our first object on the morrow should be the recovery of the escaped giant.

After breakfast, accompanied by about a dozen men, the most of whom were intended for beaters, and as many cur-dogs, we reached the scene of my rencontre the previous night. We easily discovered the foot-tracks and the broken soil that had been turned over. The former were large, but not quite as much so as I expected. We both took our stand to leeward of the cover, while the beaters with their dogs entered to windward, showing an utter disregard to thorns and briers. Their cheery voices and shouts were soon heard. A cur yelped, the others responded to the summons, and it was evident they were mobbing something. But whatever it was, it was showing fight. The confused sounds all came from the same spot, and the beaters again and again renewed their clamour.

Half an hour afterwards the beaters one by one joined us, and all concurred that a large boar was at bay. To fight the formidable animal in his lair was the only chance of success, and this we determined to do. But who was to have the honour of first risking his person in contest with the brute? I claimed it on the ground that it was unquestionably the boar I had wounded the previous night, and that, having drawn first blood, I was justly entitled to deliver the *coup de grâce*. My friend, on the other hand, argued that he might never have another similar opportunity. Like sensible men, we determined to toss, and thus decide the issue. The lot fell to me.

Divesting myself of all that might incommode me, and with nothing but my gun and hunting knife, I cautiously pushed through creepers, shrubs, and briers to where the dogs kept up their clamour. The cover was so dense that in many places I was compelled to crawl on all fours, and when doing so it was almost impossible to see ten yards in front, from the the denseness of the stems of the dwarf timber.

At length I gained a passing glance of one or two of the curs, who, with that intelligence so characteristic of all their family, recognised me at once as an ally, in proof of which they redoubled their efforts to dislodge the game.

From the increased denseness of the wood, and greater irregularity in the surface, I could only advance further on hands and knees, and that at so slow a pace as to be very tedious.

At length I was in the thick of it. The dogs rushed backward and forward, passing and re-passing each other, as if the quarry were frequently charging them; but I could not yet see the game. In front of me was a slimy moss-grown rock which rose above the surface to an irregular point. This seemed

to afford both comfortable shelter and a good
position for observation, if it could but be
gained.   Decision, on such occasions as these,
requires to be prompt, and there must be no
delay in action.

In a few moments I had gained my stand,
and was rewarded by a view of the grizzly
savage from behind it. White flakes of foam
adhered to his lips, his small eyes twinkled
with malignant hate, and he rested partially
sitting on a bed of broken and decayed *débris*,
evidently a long used nest. It was plain, from
his determined attitude, that he would fight
to the death before taking flight. The range
was but short, the target almost stationary,
my position firm and good, and I had almost
determined for a shot at the forehead ; but a
better soon offered, for a cur more plucky than
his fellows made a demonstration in rear, and
the boar turned his head to keep his assailant better in view. I, as they say in Yankee
land, " drew a bead " for that point directly
situated between the outer corner of the eye
and the root of the ear. This was but the work

of a moment, and the animal almost instantaneously fell dead.

Several hogs fell on that and the succeeding days, but none reached the magnitude of my prize. Numerous jackals also got bowled over. But although the sport was good I was tied to time, and if not punctually back within a specified date, was sure of a wigging from a not very agreeable superior. So at the hour when the flocks and herds were being led forth, we bid our hospitable hosts adieu, and turned our steps to the north-east, leaving, probably for ever, a spot that will occupy a bright place in our memories.

Our former hosts received us with pleasure. The panther had been seen in the neighbourhood the day before, and had killed a goat, which it carried off. A ravine about two miles distant was said to be its favourite retreat.

This news was sufficient to awake Smith's ardour for the chase. So after dinner, with the kid and my gun, attended by a couple of the tribe, he took his departure to the suspected locality, and did not return till break of day, completely disheartened at the continuation of his non-success, more particularly as he had fired a couple of shots at the animal he was searching for. He attributed his failure to the indifferent light; for, from being on the slope of a ravine, a heavy shadow over-hung the vicinity, and although a large animal undoubtedly passed close by him, his aim was so incorrect that he failed to bring it down. To all his entreaties to remain another night I was obliged to lend a deaf ear.

Our return journey to Bona was far from being as enjoyable as our exit from it. We had neither the pretty *vivandière* to chaff, the eccentricities of Cæsar to laugh at, nor the excitement of columns of troops constantly traversing the same route, The sun too, which had increased in power with the advance of the season, had deprived the vegetation of much of its fresh and brilliant colouring. The retreat was sounding from a dozen deep-voiced bugles, for it was evening, when we entered the straggling suburb of white, square, flat-roofed houses and gardens. Fifteen minutes more sufficed to transport us to our former quarters, where clean clothes, tubbing, shaving, and brushing made us look once more like civilized beings.

Our apartment was soon invaded by guests. Small as it was, at least twenty must have assembled in it, each bringing with him cigars, brandy, or grub. So we had a jovial night, kept well up into the "wee small hours," the roof echoing again and again to "God save the Queen," the "Star-spangled Banner" or "Partant pour la Syrie." The sober-looking Moslem neighbours must have thought us mad. One cross-grained old French field-officer did, and sent an orderly to inquire the cause of such a disturbance.

Mr. John Smith's, of Schenectady, New York, compliments, neatly indited on an envelope, were returned with a request that he would join us. The old gentleman was evidently not so black as some of his juniors had painted

him ; for a few minutes afterwards he returned an excuse for declining on the plea
of being on' duty. On the morning of our
embarkation quite a crowd attended us, and
until we had gained a distant offing, caps
and handkerchiefs could be seen waving us a
farewell, probably a long if not a final
one.

A more filthy, badly managed craft than that
in which we had taken passage for Malta probably never sailed. We were buffeted about for a
week, encountering all but very bad weather,
for which we should be thankful," ere the
friendly blaze of St. Elmo's light told us we
were off the Grand Harbour of Malta, and never
did I terminate a voyage with greater pleasure
than on this occasion.

My friend had sailed for Marseilles months
ago, and by him my photograph had gone to
that port to be posted to the *vivandière.* The
season had glided on so far that Floriana and
its gardens were baked with sun and covered over
with sand.

The migratory fashionables had all taken

their departure for more agreeable climates, and I and my brother-officers listened with pleasure to a rumour of the withdrawal of the regiment for service elsewhere—a very agreeable prospect, for the season when the sirocco blows was approaching. Purposeless and listless I had wandered one day about the ravelin of St. Frances, where we were encamped in huts, unable till late to muster sufficient energy to dress for a ride to Elmo, which I did only with the hope that the exertion and exercise would get up an appetite. My servant brought to the door my little chestnut barb, which from want of exercise was more than usually fresh.

As I cantered into the main road with slack rein, the plucky little beast showed his playful spirit by sundry buck-jumps, and as I was taking a pull on his mouth to keep him in check, I passed a *calesso* which was pulled up by the pathway. The smallest hand protruded from its door, beckoning me to stop. Who it could be I had not the slightest idea! For a moment I was vain enough to permit a fancy to cross my mind that it must be some

fair one, of the many brilliant daughters of the
sunny South, who had fallen in love with my
gallant self, and, regardless of consequences,
had determined, in this manner, to obtain an
interview with me and at the same time keep
her intrigue unknown. Many will exclaim: What
a puppy the fellow must be! No indeed!
not more so than the rest of his race and
sex. Vanity is generally largely developed in
them, particularly before they reach the age
of five-and-twenty, and have adopted arms as
their profession.

As I turned about and approached the conveyance, I no doubt drew myself up and
assumed my most killing looks, while, in
imagination, I pictured the *incognita* as a
Haydee in form and grace. While indulging
in these freaks of fancy, the door of the *calesso* opened, and out stepped—not the fairy
sylph-like form I had painted in my mind—no
dark brunette with almond eyes that read
your deepest thoughts at sight, but—whom
would you suppose?—my mother! In a moment
I was in her arms.

Truly, reader, I was not one whit disappointed, but certainly much surprised, for I believed her to be at home; and as she was well on in years, and not addicted to travelling, she was of all persons certainly the last I expected to see. How she came to be in a *calesso*, and halted by the road side, is soon explained.

This was the first conveyance that presented itself on landing, and the dear old lady knew not that the island possessed others. She had engaged its driver to take her to the camp, and on arriving at the entrance he had proceeded on foot to inquire for me, while my mother remained seated. In the meantime, I had left, and our meeting had taken place as described.

But what had induced the old lady to come so far, many will exclaim. The fact was, my escapade with the *vivandière* had, through Smith, been magnified into a genuine love-affair, and the present of my picture seemed to confirm this view of the case. A dowdy old major, a friend of the family, therefore thought it his duty to inform the worthy *mater*, and she had hastened off, resting neither day nor night till she was by her boy's side, to prevent, what she considered, a dreadful *mésalliance*. But mothers will be mothers, and when they err it is from want of judgment, not from sincerity of motives. Thus ended my shooting trip to Algeria.

CHAPTER X.

How Money is made in America—*Ne Sutor ultra Crepidam* —Fall in the Value of Stock—New and Accessible Shooting Ground—Variety and Abundance of Game—The Breech-loader *v.* Muzzle-loader—Terriers and Wild Cat—Fat Stock —Accidents from Want of Caution with Cattle.

RETURNING from the azure seas and sunny skies of the Mediterranean to a country not less attractive, time passed rapidly in my friend's society, and, when the day for his departure came, it was with regret at his leaving that I drove him to the railway station.

As an example of how money is sometimes made in this country, I will state that my late visitor found himself, at his father's death, possessed of an immense tract of wild land, worth, at the utmost valuation, about four dollars per acre. Among the numerous railways which were constructed about twelve years ago, one was run directly through the centre of his estate, and a station built upon its limits. A town soon sprung up around it, and property increased in value to such an extent that what had been previously valueless prairie now yields an almost princely revenue. Such instances in America are too numerous to create surprise, for there is not a State in the Union in which numerous similar instances cannot be cited.

An accident occurred to my big chestnut horse, which caused me much annoyance. John, the sailor, whom I have previously mentioned, having been installed master of the horse, received orders to harness my late purchase to the market-waggon. This he performed before placing the bridle on the horse's head. A sudden alarm being raised among the animals in the farm-yard, the chestnut horse took fright, dashed across the enclosure, and attempted to jump a gate at the further end. In this effort he succeeded, but left the trap shattered in pieces behind him.

For hours the runaway could not be found, but at length I discovered him in the centre of the prairie, miles from home, divested of every vestige of harness except his collar. The poor frightened creature was in such a state of excitement that he stood panting as if his heart would burst, being almost incapable of further exertion. I knew he was ruined for harness purposes.

Such a fright as he had just received, no young horse would ever get over; and to make a long story short, he was sold for a song. My castle in the air was thus ruthlessly tumbled down, for up to the date of the accident he had progressed so favourably that I had already declined to part with him for almost double the sum I had paid for him. One lesson, however, I learned, that, however skilful sailors may be in reefing topsails, and making knots and splices, they are not suitable for grooms.

Poor John! After the first blow up, I said no more to him, for his good honest face spoke how keenly he felt being the cause of my loss.

The position of the Confederacy, meanwhile, has become so critical that provisions of all descriptions are rapidly decreasing in price, so much so that if I were now to sell my stock of cattle they would not realize sufficient to cover the outlay. Still I hold on to them in the hope that some unforeseen circumstance may cause a re-action in the market. My stock, I believe, looked so well that I almost disliked parting with them, knowing that soon afterwards their fate would be the slaughter-house. Although it was almost a moral certainty that I should be a heavy loser by my drove, I could not help thinking that in more prosperous times, there could be few lives more enjoyable than that of a stock-raiser in this charming country.

The following letter I received from a friend. From the valuable information it contains, in reference to a new and certainly most accessible shooting-ground near Brookfield, State of Missouri, I produce it intact :—

" Our experience has been so satisfactory that we all concur in feeling indebted to Mr. ——— for the excellence of our sport. In the course of some years' experience—in which I have visited nearly all of the Northwestern States in pursuit of game—never have I come across ground so admirably suited for shooting. The diversity and unevenness of the ground, the equal division between prairie and timber, the numerous creeks and ponds, are exactly what a millionaire would form, if intent on constructing a gigantic preserve.

" Game was really abundant—wonderfully so —and instead of pursuing our course further, as had been previously intended, we were satisfied to remain until our spare time expired, and had no reason to regret this change of mind. The variety of game was great, an immense point in adding to the pleasure. I should always prefer a more moderate mixed bag to a heavier one of all the same kind.

"We picked up quite a number of woodcock, and are assured at certain seasons of the year they are quite numerous. This is probable, for the soil and cover look well adapted for the feeding of the long bills, and I know by experience that this bird is to be found in immense quantities on the shores and islands of the Upper Mississippi.

"The prairie-chickens were far from being as wild as might be expected so late in the fall, perhaps because they have been so little shot at, or, more probably, from the irregular, hilly surface, which will frequently allow you to approach close on their resting place without coming into sight. Partridge, on the edge of the openings and in the vicinity of cultivation, absolutely swarm, and anyone who would devote a day to them alone, if only a tolerable shot, could bag an immense number ere the sun set.

"On some ponds a few miles off we saw a number of wild geese, but they were shy. As these ponds are fed by springs which do not easily freeze, and there is abundance of cover in their vicinity, on the approach of hard weather good sport might doubtless be obtained at them. The beautiful little woodcock we found numerous, and although I never can kill one without regret in depriving so handsome a bird of life, my companions were not loth to try their skill, and consequently we frequently had them on our table.

"The canvas-back in our Eastern States is highly prized for its delicacy of flavour, but I think many of our Western duck are quite as fine. In Baltimore and vicinity such an assertion would be deemed heresy, but my shoulders are broad enough to bear the brunt, even if I were far less distant from the Monumental City.

"With the march of improvemnt, small bore guns have greatly gone out, and I find "ten" more popular than "fourteen." My old companion, a "fourteen," I have determined to lay up in ordinary, and have one of the larger size. Now comes the point which I want your advice upon : Shall it be a muzzle or a breech-loader ? Your experience and knowledge shall decide. The latter I have never used, but report speaks favourably, and several are in use among my friends.

"Cocking spaniels I am determined to have for next season, and as soon as I can get a friend to join me in the project, will import two brace. I should fear to bring less, for accident might deprive me of the chance of propagating the breed.

"Some of our sporting celebrities are seriously canvassing the propriety of a trip to the plains, next season, for buffalo. Could you join us if an invitation were extended? You would have less to fear than the majority, as it would be difficult to raise *your hair*. I cannot provide you with a correct return of our game bag, for all were too indolent or too intent on other work to keep record. Of this you may be satisfied, that it was heavy—I may say very."

In the latter portion of this letter will be found a question interesting to all, whether I should recommend the breech in preference to the muzzle-loader. For months I have been puzzling my brains on this very question, and yet remain undecided. Strange to say this morning I have written to my gun-maker, Mr. Dougall, of St. James's Street, London, for advice upon the subject, and as I have ever found him a most reliable and conscientious person, I shall be entirely controlled by it.

When in China a few years ago I purchased a "Lefaucheux," but a weaker shooting gun I never possessed. This may have prejudiced me against the new arm, but breech-loaders were then, comparatively speaking, in their infancy.

A little episode worthy of mention has just been reported to me by Kelly, and from the appearance of the terriers I believe he has in no way exaggerated.

While in the woods this morning he was attracted by the incessant barking of the dogs. On going to learn the cause, he discovered a wild cat in a detached sapling. Having shaken the tree the cat sprang to the ground, and was instantly seized by Tip, Topsy and Tiney without delay coming to his assistance. They had, however, no easy foe to deal with, and would only have come off second best but for Kelly's assistance. The cat weighed twenty-one pounds.

Who would believe that the fat, sleek, good-looking drove of cattle I inspected to-day were the starvlings that I helped to drive home some months since? Their coats now were looking as smooth and glossy as if they were regularly groomed; while their eyes stood forth bright and clear, emblematic of health. How changed too are their proportions, for the prominent bones have disappeared, and the flat flanks have given way to well developed paunches! Their life certainly appears a happy one, for, with the exception of keeping their tails going, to whisk off the bloodthirsty horse-flies and mosquitos, they have nothing to do but to help themselves to the nutritious herbage that in places grows in such rank profusion as to reach their stomachs.

With prosperity they are also becoming saucy, and there are several members of the drove that it would not be judicious to approach on foot. When on horseback, however, there is nothing to fear, for man and horse together are evidently associated in their minds as something irresistible, more especially if your appearance should be heralded by the cracking of your stock-whip, which, in the hands of a dismounted man would not have half the moral influence over their behaviour. It is the combination does it, added to the memory of past experiences. The bullock that will toss his head and paw the ground when you approach him on foot, will fly like the wind, and all the herd that are near him will join in the stampede, if you approach mounted and armed with the lash. But as a rule, I think cattle are not nearly so dangerous here as they are at home.

This doubtless results from early education, Still accidents do occasionally happen, one of which was reported the other day. A bull which had previously been most exemplary in its conduct was confined in a paddock, through the centre of which was a path used by the neighbours from being deemed a short cut.

An old woman who was returning from market selected this route to reach her home. Unfortunately she was habited in a red or scarlet cloak, which, as everyone knows has a most exciting influence upon many animals, horned cattle in particular. The victim had got half way over when the bull spied her. At first the animal only slowly approached her, but the old woman, becoming terrified, bolted for the exit of the field, and in her efforts to gain it missed her footing and fell.

The pursuer, who was in a moment upon her, made a pass at her with his horns and seriously bruised the unfortunate woman, at the same time dragging her cloak off her back. Luckily it got entangled in his horns, and all his tossing could not relieve him of the scarlet object which continued dangling and flapping about his eyes and head, till he became so irritated that, bellowing with rage he rushed about the field, cutting every imaginable caper to free himself from it. The old lady at once picked herself up, and lost no time in placing a safe distance between herself and her assailant. If it had not been for the cloak attaching itself to the bull's horns, she very probably would have been killed.

CHAPTER XI.

Stock Driving—Chevaline Sympathy—Pleasant Retreat—The Squirrel's Store-room—Mementoes of a Past Race—Fall of Prices in the Cattle Market—Sale of my Stock.

IT is extraordinary how some horses become so accustomed to stock-driving that they will almost perform the work without any assistance from the rider. We have an old mare called Jinny, possessed of only one eye (but that a thoroughly good one) which when employed in driving will do almost all the work. If a heifer or steer be refractory, she will lay hold of its flank with her teeth, and in more instances than one she has been known to bite out the piece!

In my sundry wanderings about the neighbourhood in search of game or picturesque scenery, I had discovered a retreat on the banks of the Embaras. It was a charming nook, carpeted with the softest grass and surrounded on three sides by handsome spreading trees. To the south it was guarded by the rippling river. I had often resolved to pay this spot a visit, and as frequently circumstances had prevented my carrying my intention into effect; but to-day being without visitors and free from business duties, I determined to carry out my often postponed resolution and have a long interrupted chat with memory.

How often have I observed my horse affected by my own feelings! There is no doubt that, through animal magnetism, the rider transfers to his steed the dominant sensations of the moment. Fanny was dull and lethargic as we threaded our way through the timber that skirted the edge of the farm, so much so in fact did her thoughts appear to wander that she struck against several roots and stumps, tripping so heavily as almost to imperil her knees. At length an unusually serious stumble recalled me from dream-land, when, taking her well in hand, I reminded her that I wore spurs, and at a good hand-gallop struck across the prairie to the place I had selected for my retreat.

Tying the mare to a sapling, I proceeded to the water's edge, and took my seat upon a rock that slightly overhung the passing stream. Behind my position was an eddy, where particles of vegetation chased each other in miniature circles, and among this circling refuse played hundreds of minnows. These bright, happy, restless creatures appeared a hungry lot, rushing at and struggling over any tempting food that happened to be washed into the eddy out of the parent stream.

When a fly or other insect dropped upon the surface within their domain, its life was terminated in a moment, and it was dismembered into innumerable pieces, which fell into as many tiny jaws as could obtain hold of them. What little tyrants these silvery beauties were, how blood-thirsty! No quarter did they give, no remorse of conscience did they feel. One text alone appeared

known to them. Slay and devour, slay and
devour.

But their life was not all sunshine. There
were dark spots on the sky of their career;
for while all the population of the eddy appeared enjoying themselves to the utmost,
restlessly and perpetually moving like figures
in an intricate dance, a dark monster would
dash in amongst them, and in a moment the
happy crowd would be dispersed. A large
black-bass, with an unfortunate minnow
in his mouth, would then be seen leisurely
retiring into the more rapid and deeper
water.

But the tragedy just enacted among these
tiny residents of the river failed to teach
them a lesson of caution, for in a few
minutes all were back to their favourite haunt,
enjoying their usual sport, and their lost companion was forgotten: an image of what we
see every day among humanity. The pride of
a mess-table, the flower of a wide circle of
friends, is removed to another world, but still the
colours are trooped as previously, and parties,

dances, and pleasures are enjoyed as heretofore.

Near the edge of this eddy grew some lotus
plants. So still and smooth was the surface
of the water around them that they had failed
to attract more than a cursory look; but
they were well worthy of observation, for
among them was hid a reptile intent on repeating the performance of the black-bass; but
of his presence I was ignorant, till a sudden
splash on the surface of the water attracted
my attention, and revealed the lurking marauder.

In an hour he repeated this manœuvre successfully more than a dozen times, till, becoming disgusted with the snake's insatiable greed,
I rid the locality of his presence by a well-
directed blow. To gratify my curiosity I
opened his stomach, and counted among its
contents no less than fifteen minnows, not one
of which was in the slightest state of decom-
position! I also discovered a pulpy, half-con-
sumed piece of animal matter, which, from
certain indications, I should say formed part

of a live frog the day before. Though "live and let live" is a motto often preached by us, I fear we no more practise it than do the snakes, black-bass, or minnows.

Behind where I had sat for the last half hour, a regular magging match of squirrels had been going on. The old gin-drinking harridans of Clare Market could not keep up one of their controversies with more energy. I am perfectly aware who the originators of the disturbance are, and should not have now turned my attention to them, but that their persistent chattering implies that they must be about business of greater importance than officers usually have when under the plea of "urgent private affairs" they apply for leave of absence.

A cautious change of my position brought the controversialists within range of sight, and what a state of hurry, bustle, and excitement they were in! Judging from my knowledge of animal life, these ground-squirrels prognosticated a rapid change of weather; the approach of the frosts and snows of Winter, before which it was imperative for them to complete, without delay, the store of provisions necessary for that inclement season.

This Tamias is a charming little creature, peculiar to the woods of North America. It is nearly as large as our red squirrel, but is of a beautiful bright fawn colour, with two dark stripes longitudinally running along the back on either side of the vertebræ. Not being by nature timid, they are frequently seen; their agility, beauty, and confidence winning the admiration of all. First one of this trium-virate would dart off into the bush, to return with equal promptness; his cheek pouches distended to their utmost, for in them are the stores it is carrying to the garner. In a moment it would disappear into its retreat, to return rapidly, when it would sit up on its hind legs and chatter to the others—these answering before the first speaker was per-mitted to have his say out.

If I had been skilled in their language, I have not the slightest doubt I should have learned that a splendid hickory nut, or equally desirable hazel nut, had been found and added to their stock of provisions. It is not impossible that information was afforded that there were plenty more to be found where the last came from. In fact, I think this very probable, for after their powers of conversation became exhausted all three scampered into the brush, and after a short delay returned loaded. The store-room of the ground-squirrels was in a little mound of earth, which might have been raised either by the hand of man, or by the rubbish which adheres to the root of a decayed tree. The former appeared to me the most probable, as there remained no stump or decayed log in its immediate vicinity.

Having procured a strong stake, I commenced excavating around the entrance to the granary. The ground was soft, and I made rapid progress. In half an hour I had reached the store-room, and in it found almost a capful of nuts, the greater number of which were pecans, the most delicate flavoured and consequently most valued of all the walnut family.

Some Indian corn and wheat was also among the stores, this most probably being gathered from among the wash on the river side, for to my knowledge neither of these cereals flourished within several miles of where I then was. It was too bad to rob the harmless little innocents of the results of their labour, and so they thought; for if length and emphasis may be accepted as a criterion, such a scolding I never received before for severity.

I had however an object to gain, namely, an insight into the economy of their lives, which might be utilized at a future period. Not only did I obtain this insight, but reaped even a greater reward, by finding several Indian arrow-heads, as perfect in shape and sharp on the edges as they were the day when the aborigines constructed them. These mementoes of a past race told 'me that it was a grave in which I was digging, not unlikely the resting place of a great chief or warrior; for it was only with males of distinction that arms were buried, and the situation, from my knowledge of the Red man's habits, was exactly the place that would have been selected for a person of no mean standing among his tribe. I penetrated deeper into the loose mould, but my perseverance was rewarded only by the discovery of the head of an old clay pipe, which on inspection did not indicate great age. I concluded therefore that the tenant of this secluded and lovely resting place had been taken to the spirit-land not over a century, but probably within a shorter period

The pipe plays an important part in all the ceremonies of the Indians, whether war or peace be the cause of the gathering of the braves, whether the election of a chief or the decoration of distinguished warriors. The pipe is invariably handed round as a prelude to their deliberations, and it again circulates at the conclusion of their assembly. This pipe had possibly been used on such occasions. Perhaps it had touched the lips of men as brave as ever drew a bow, or had belonged to one at whose bidding a thousand dusky warriors were ever willing and ready to take the war path. Alas ! where are their people now ? What has become of their descendants ? They are obliterated from the

face of the earth, through the grasping greed
and avarice of the white man. They have
scarcely left a trace to perpetuate their memory!

[I sat one evening on the margin of a western
lake of Minnesota. The day had been bright
and charming, and having had a long day's
tramp in pursuit of game, I now felt it necessary
to enjoy a little rest. The spot that I had
reached was eminently suited to my purpose, a
grassy bank rising so abruptly as to afford an
extensive view. I sat down at the summit of
the acclivity, on what I afterwards discovered
to be a grave; possibly from absence of mind I
was ignorant at the time that such it was. I
sat facing the sun, which was setting over the
clear transparent water in all the glory of
colour peculiar to this western land.

A movement near disturbed me, and turning
to discover the intruder, I saw an Indian leaning
on his rifle. There was a sad expression on his
countenance as he gazed on me, and with as
much kindness as I could assume, I asked him
his purpose, at the same time requesting him

to join me in my rest. Receiving no answer to this invitation, I filled my pipe, lit it and presented it to him; but he waved it off with a dignity worthy of a monarch refusing to accept the price of his people's blood.

"I am your friend," I said, "why do you refuse to smoke with me?"

"Because," and his eyes flashed, "your race is the destroyer of mine, you and yours own my inheritance, and even now you desecrate my father's grave. Can you not rest satisfied of your power, without disturbing the resting place of him your people killed when he was defending his own."

"But I had nothing to do with this, I belong not to this country," was my reply.

His answer, however, was to the purpose. "You do not, neither do any of them. You come from the East, so have all the Pale-faces. Yours is the land of the rising, ours of the setting sun. Our sun has set, yours has risen; but it cannot always be in the heavens, there must be a night for you as well as for us."

Having thus spoken he disappeared, his last words still echoing in my ears when the brush had shut out all trace of his retreating figure. What he said was just and true. How could he accept a favour from one of a race that had nearly exterminated his tribe?]

As night approached I sought my pony. The little pet welcomed me with a neigh. The winds were sighing dismally through the trees, the harsh grating of their limbs producing with each successive gust sounds that harmonized in every respect with a landscape so depressing in its influence upon the mind. I tried to fly from the gloomy thoughts that assailed me; but even the speed of my horse was not swift enough to accomplish this purpose.

That night Winter paid its first visit, and in the morning, when I saw his stamp upon the earth, I thought with grief over the poor little ground-squirrels I had robbed. Possibly my mis-appropriation of their property caused their death, just as the mis-appropriation of the Indian's hunting lands has been their destruction.

A perfect crash has occurred in the cattle-market, there being no further demand for commissariat stores, on account of the disbandment of the Volunteer Army. The prices that were paid for provisions during the war have ceased, and cattle and grain have reverted to even less than their original value, or to about one-third of the prices they fetched a few months since; and worse than all, as far as human foresight can form an estimate, it is more than probable that years will have to pass before a reaction occurs to increase their value. I have, therefore, resolved to part with my herd, a step that I much regret, but for which there is no alternative; for although the animals cost little to feed, yet a certain number of losses must occur from disease or accident.

Several purchasers have been to look at the herd, but I treated with scorn all their attempts to buy, for their offers appeared to me far beneath the value of my stock. Waiting, however, has not improved matters, and I have accepted for my favourites one-fourth less money than they cost me a year back. So much for speculation! I have burnt my fingers, but this must be accepted as an exceptional case; for I feel convinced that under ordinary circumstances, at a time when there is no war panic, I should be a handsome gainer by raising or feeding live stock.

After all it was rather a gambling transaction, for I played for a heavy stake—not for ordinary profit. The actual result is only such as should have been looked forward to as within the range of possibility.

Whatever, however, may have been my own luck in stock-dealing, I believe that a handsome and certain income can be made by it in this portion of Illinois with little labour and anxiety, for Nature never adapted a country better for the purpose. Anyone who proposes to embark in such an enterprise had better not delay, for it cannot be long ere the rich lands on the Wabash will all be fenced in, and utilized for more valuable purposes than stock-raising.

Some of my readers may be inclined to ask, how much capital would be required by an emigrant gentleman to start in this country with a fair prospect of success? My answer is that with one thousand pounds a man must be a fool who does not make a sufficiency and to spare. As far as hard work goes, all required of a settler would be a pleasant and natural interest in his own affairs. The great drawback to the educated in Transatlantic life is the difficulty of procuring good servants, but it makes one self-reliant, and imposes the necessity of exercise, when one would probably be indulging in the morbid feelings which spring from idleness. Why should a man not clean his own boots, as before to-day he has groomed his own horse, or washed out his own gun? No greater objections can be urged against the one than against the others.

In favour of America there is one important point I must urge—in fact I should do injustice to the land in which I spent so many happy days if I neglected it, namely, the uniform hospitality and kindness of its people; for if you meet them but half way, which I fear new arrivals seldom do, they will assist you by every possible means, even to the extent of freely drawing in your favour the strings of their purses, if that should be necessary, to save you trouble or anxiety. Objectionable persons are, no doubt, to be found in the land of the West, but they are the exception, not the rule.

The distinction of classes is not known here as at home, and tradespeople occupy the highest standing in society; but if your baker, grocer, and upholsterer are good fellows, gentlemanly in their deportment, and possessed of such qualities as you appreciate in a companion, why, in the name of goodness, should you not associate with them? Because they manufacture the bread you eat, import the teas or coffees you drink, or make the chairs and sofas you lounge upon, do not appear to me sufficient reasons why you should deny yourself the pleasure of associating with those who probably may be mentally your superiors. In circumstances of difficulty, danger, or hardship, it is wonderful how soon rank is sunk, and the best man obtains supremacy; not that for a moment I wish to suggest that the best-bred person is not also the one who shines preeminently in adversity.

It must not be forgotten, also, that, in America, "one man in his time plays many parts." The lawyer or trader of to-day may be the soldier of to-morrow. The counsellor (barrister) exchanges places with the judge, the judge with the counsellor. Hereditary rank being unknown, men go honestly into any speculation that will pay, and close observers may have noticed a tendency to the same levelling practice of late years in Great Britain, to the great advantage of all ranks of society.

CHAPTER XII.

FROM my long association with the military
profession I seldom allowed an opportunity of
viewing troops to pass without availing myself
of it. Curiosity may in some measure account
for this, but not to the same extent as a desire
which I felt to compare the soldiery of one
nation with those of another, with the view
of observing their capabilities of service if
they should ever be summoned to meet each
other in hostile array.

The United States' regular army is principally

composed of foreigners; but, this force being numerically small, it is unnecessary to say more of it than that it is in the highest possible state of discipline. That vast volunteer force, however, which flooded the country at the period of the secession of the Southern States deserves more than a passing remark. Those corps of voluntary soldiers raised in the Eastern States had their ranks swelled by the enlistment of men from every part of Europe; while those of the Western States were for the most part American-bred citizens. With the former I had little to do; but I was well acquainted with the latter, and will confine my remarks principally to them.

In Illinois and Indiana the rural population turned out *en masse* to support their country in its great struggle, the feelings with which they espoused her cause amounting to enthusiasm. The powerful frames and hardy constitutions of men accustomed to endure all manner of hardships and fatigue from their infancy, were the materials from which was produced a

body of soldiers who could nowhere be sur-
passed.

Their temper was proved by the long marches
and the almost impossible deeds which they
performed. In one essential, however, they
were wanting, namely, discipline—a deficiency
which was in some measure made up for by
esprit de corps, and in the course of time was
to a great extent remedied, although slowly,
which is not surprising when we consider the
early education and training of these republican sons of the soil. One advantage they
all possessed at the moment of their enlistment, an intimate acquaintance with the use
of fire-arms, and a thorough reliance on their
own capacity of handling them in the most effec-
tive manner.

These Western residents thus possessed a
great superiority over the promiscuous bands
collected from different European nations, most
of whom had to learn the use of the rifle, which,
if one wishes to become a perfect shot, must, I
believe, be acquired at an early age.

Dobbin and Giles, who had never handled a gun, necessarily required a long period of tuition before they obtained even a moderate dexterity in its use; while Jonathan and Hans, as soon as they were called from their homesteads, made efficient skirmishers or irregular troops.

With physique, shrewdness, and a thorough knowledge of fire-arms to start with, can it be deemed a matter of surprise that these troops, under such a general as Sherman, rapidly marched through the heart of their enemy's country, and successfully resisted all the efforts of the foe to arrest their progress?

The want of discipline must necessarily be regarded by military men as one of the most serious obstacles to the success of an army; but in America it has scarcely the same meaning as in Europe, for in the New World it implies principally an inability on the part of the officers to restrain the ardour of their men, not to induce them to advance. After all, however, a disciplined army cannot be

made in a few months, or even in a year or
two, particularly when it is serving in its own
land.   These Transatlantic troops, transported
into a hostile country, where they might expect an enemy on every side, would, for the
sake of mutual protection, soon learn to rely
on one another, and submit without hesitation
to the commands of their superiors.

Few general readers are not aware that
there are large and numerous settlements of
Germans   throughout . the   Western   States.
With the natural loyalty of their people,
they promptly responded to the call of the
Federal Government for volunteers.   Thus numerous regiments, composed entirely of the
children of the Fatherland, were summoned to
the field.

The genuine American is much in the
habit of sneering at the Dutchman (as all
Germans are familiarly called); but when it
was known how steadily they fought, how un-
complainingly they endured hardships, and how
well they behaved, whether in the face of the
foe or in cantonments among friends, they rose

in the estimation of the people of their adopted country to the position which they ever deserved, and should have from the first enjoyed, but that necessity had never demanded an exhibition of their true worth.

I have seen the troops of nearly every European nation, and have served in the field with several of them; and although my opinions may not be deemed of much value, I can unhesitatingly say that the United States possess a population from which can be obtained soldiers inferior to none in the world.

But to return to less serious matters. Time has lately hung very heavily on my hands, because, so far as field-sports are concerned, it is a season not distinguished by any characteristic marks, and country life without them always appears to me slow in the extreme. I therefore hailed with delight a report that a Prairie wolf had made its appearance in the neighbourhood, committing depredations so numerous that its destruction became imperative.

A Prairie wolf is not a large animal, for it does not exceed the height and bulk of an undersized setter ; but its capacity for mischief is very gre̊at, and it shows an insatiable love of blood which is truly marvellous. One of these pests will sometimes kill many sheep in one night, for when its prey is abundant it becomes so fastidious that it rejects the mutton and is only satisfied with blood. Dogs that like highway-men take to the country to obtain a living, are equally destructive of sheep, eating only the most delicate tid-bits. As no one from whom I sought information could say that he had seen the despoiler, I could not help believing that he would turn out to be a *ci-devant* friend of man, instead of a representative of the Lupus family.

The scratch pack of hounds which the neigh-bourhood boasted of had several times been mustered, in the hope of a run that would put a termination to the farmers' complaints ; but although every cover, swamp, and rush-mar-gined slough had been drawn, not a trace could be discovered of the animal we sought. Though this was very discouraging, to say the least of it, yet the number of horsemen who desired to participate in the destruction of the wily foe did not in the least diminish, but rather increased.

I have no doubt, however, that the chat by the cover side, the gallop from one draw to another, or the excuse for imbibing more than a usual amount of whiskey, were the inducements which drew out a great many—a pack of hounds in this neighbourhood never having previously had so goodly an attendance.

Returning one evening from one of these unsuccessful runs, it was decided, without dissent, that another attempt should be made in a day or two, when the work would commence by drawing the swamp where I had my adventure with the wild pigs; and afterwards, if we did not then succeed in finding the object of our search, by hunting the river margin that lay to the north of my house. It was a glorious morning that ushered in the day when this programme was to be followed—just such a one as would delight the heart of the most fastidious foxhunter—so that all hoped, if we got away upon anything like fair terms with our quarry, we should either force him to succumb, or drive him from the neighbourhood.

Kelly, who never could go to work when any sport was in prospect, if there was a chance of his absence remaining undiscovered, came to me, with a most serio-comic air, for the loan of the little mare, " Jist that he might see a bit of the spree." To this I gave assent, for she was an old screw, with scarcely a leg to stand upon ; but with as much go in her, if she could be kept on her pins, as many equally antiquated pieces of horse-flesh that all have known in the course of their lives.

There are few military men who were stationed in Canada a matter of five or six years back who will not remember Charley Riley and Nannie Craddock.   Neither of them had much to boast of as far as the soundness of their limbs went, yet both were race-horses.   The old mare I lent to Kelly was their contemporary in age, and little inferior in speed, bottom, and jumping powers.   In fact with ten and a-half stone on her back she could go the pace and show her tail to any ordinary hunt ; and the rider who was going to cross her was under that weight, with pluck, seat, and hands that had gained him a reputation among the hard-riding members of one of the crack packs of the Emerald Island. I made up my mind therefore that, if a run should ensue and a new line of country be taken, I would play follow-my-leader to the gallant little Irishman.

Such a heterogeneous lot as assembled at my house that morning would have provoked to mirth all who had a knowledge of the punctilious care with which such details are carried out in England. The eye-witness, however, must have been a veritable cynic if he did not at once perceive that the day's proceedings promised abundance of fun.

Tony, the Dutchman, in his rotund proportions, was mounted on a galloway that would have done good service in a dray. A late Prussian officer bestrode a gigantic trotter, as if on parade. A number of shopkeepers appeared on animals that did duty in their delivery carts. Farmers rode to the rendezvous on their plough-horses, and a nigger exhibited himself on an ill-tempered badly formed mule !

The meet altogether was of such a character as could have been formed only from the motley population of a Western state. Jumping powder is in use here as well as across the Atlantic, and no doubt a good many doses of that physic had been swallowed by each sportsman that morning before starting.

At length the horn of the huntsman "too-tooed" the start, which all obeyed after receiving a caution not to over-ride the pack of —— fox hounds, I was going to say curs. It was, as I have said, a glorious morning, the wind soft and pleasant, the light subdued, and the vegetable world arrayed in many gorgeous colours.

Nothing of importance occurred before we reached our cover, if I except the circumstance that the darkie on the mule got a tremendous spill; some playful practical joker having inserted a corn-cob between the animal's back and the seat of the saddle. Niggers, however, are generally considered fair game for sport, and the son of Africa did not, judging from the grin that covered his ebony countenance as he arose from Mother Earth, appear to express any vindictiveness at this practical joke.

The swamp, as heretofore, was drawn blank, the more impatient murmuring that we could only expect a repetition of our usual luck—a prediction which proved them to be false prophets, for immediately afterwards, in a wild plum and hazel grove that grew in the vicinity, and margined the Prairie, every hound opened with a burst of vehemence that left no doubt that the game was on foot.

What a scampering and racing immediately afterwards ensued for the open land! And this energy was even redoubled when Kelly's voice, singing out loudly " gone away," was borne to our ears. The copse was soon cleared, and the pack were streaming over a rise in the Prairie, with their heads up and sterns down, as if in view of their quarry, while their various voices reverberated unceasingly from the timber. This looked like a realization of our hopes, and happily the line of country selected was, for good riding, the most promising that could have been chosen.

Wishing to save my horse thus early in the game, for I had reason to believe that a heavy job was before him, I satisfied myself by whipping up the tail of the hunt. For a couple of miles all had been plain sailing, but now we approached a farm partitioned off with deep ditches and post-and-rail fences. Kelly was the first to reach it, and he popped over it like a bird, while the old mare gave the boards a slap with her heels and told how proficient she was at timber-fencing.

The ease with which the first fence had been disposed of by the Irishman doubtless gave courage to his followers, for, to the credit of all, not one refused the lead; but their pluck deserved better reward than was accorded them, for never in my experience did I see so many people unhorsed in so small a space; the one person who got safe over being the nigger, and he only did so after his mule had played at sea-saw over the impediment for some seconds, during which it remained doubtful whether it would advance or retire. The top-board, however, finally breaking down under the combined weight and motion of the animal, opened an admirable gap for me.

It was a rich scene to look along that fence. In the majority of instances, riders and mounts were on different sides of it. Some retained their reins, while others wistfully gazed after their nags, which, rejoicing in their freedom, were scampering off in the direction of their homes. A little French doctor, whom I almost rode over on entering the field, and who still remained seated just as he had fallen, gazed up in my face as I passed.

A faint but prolonged exclamation from him reached my ear. I am not certain, for I would not wish to asperse any man's character, but I am under the impression it was a Gallic oath.

The sport had, as yet, only commenced; the wolf not having gone straight away, for the hunt took us backwards and forwards, and round about; and on all occasions, where the stiffest jumping was to be done, there was Kelly at the tail of the hounds, doing his work as if he were not out of his teens, and the mare he straddled still in her prime. I had no desire to compete with him for honours, but was willing to be satisfied with a good place, and that I had. All my efforts, however, failed, even in so open a country, to obtain a "view halloo."

By this time, those who had not parted company from their nags commenced to make their appearance, by bisecting short cuts; but I observed that all, save the nigger on the mule, showed a marked objection to timber, ditches, and everything that required a jump. In and out, back and forth, we went. Never did hare, in my knowledge, run such a tortuous course. The hounds, however, experienced no difficulty in unravelling it, but pushed forward with unabated ardour.

Several times Kelly had sung out the " view halloo," but somehow or other my eyes refused to endorse his statement; in fact, I had begun to "smell a mice," as a celebrated Dutchman said, and concluded we were running a drag, although several of the hunt had stated that they had unquestionably seen the wolf at the time he broke cover.

The finish of the run was towards home, and strange to say, the termination took place within a stone's throw of my house, where, although a dozen casts were made, not an acknowledgment could be obtained of the direction the pursued had afterwards taken. Various were the suggestions offered to account for this phenomenon; but when a gentleman more enthusiastic than his fellows, or more interested in wool-growing than any one present, proposed to cut down a cotton-wood tree, almost four feet in diameter, which sloped at an angle of forty-five degrees, in a cavity of which the marauder was supposed to be hid, I decamped for home, taking all with me who were thirsty.

Strange to say, so numerous were those

troubled with this appetite, that none remained to unravel the mystery of where the Prairie wolf had secreted himself.

Before my friends left in the evening, I learned from one of them that Harris, whose ungrateful and ruffianly conduct I have recorded, and whom I had immediately discharged, had notoriously associated himself with a band of swindlers and horse-stealers. As the eyes of the police were on this nest of robbers, whose plans and haunts were becoming known, I was assured that my old friend's career would in all probability be a short one, and I believe this assertion was verified not long afterwards.

CHAPTER XIII.

IT is seldom that a week passes without strolling troops of negro minstrels visiting the vicinity. The genuine Sambo is always considered here the essence of low comedy, yet during the late war few of this race were treated as comic characters. That, however, does not prevent the performers, darkened with black cork, from being more popular than any others who provide the public with amusement.

The following is a specimen of their style of fun, which, for meaningless absurdity, much resembles that of their *confrères* in England :—

" *Interlocutor.*—Mr. Bones, I was going to ask you something, but I'll postpone the question, for here comes Brother Cusick, with his banjo over his shoulder, and the strings all broken, and he looks as if he'd been having a row with somebody.

[*Enter Sam Cusick, dejectedly.*

" *Int.*—How now, Brother Cusick? You seemed plunged in melancholy.

" *Cusick.*—Dat what you call it? I bin plunged into a pile o' *slacked lime*—dat's what's de matter! Got into de fust railroad car I cum across to come ober to de hall, but de 'ductor didn't 'preciate music, so he ducked me in de lime puddle, an' I made a hoss *collar* ober de head of a man wid my banjo, trying to git out.

" *Int.*— Indeed. That must have provoked *your choler*, and I don't wonder you showed *horse*-tility.

" *Cusick.*—You bet it did! Tore off de only *collar* I had, and de shirt near cum wid it. But I got even.

" *Int.*—You got even?

" *Cusick.*—I did dat. I went into de dry goods store dat de lime belong to, I was so mad, and sitting down on de *sol fa*—

" *Int.*—The *sofa*, you mean, sir.

" *Cusick.*—Well, de *so far*; I ax for de boss, and says I, right amongst all de ladies, says I:— 'Bossy, don't you want to get a genteel clerk here, bossy? I'll come cheap.' 'Then you're just the feller I don't want,' says he. 'It 'd take half my stock to refit you.' And I went out, leaving a broad streak of whitewash behind me. If he did reject me, it couldn't a bin on de 'count of my *color*.

" *Int.*—That was evident. Well, sir, what did you do next?

" *Cusick.* — I went ober to de offis ob de *Mornin' Rostrum* to state de facts ob de case and demand satisfaction.

" *Int.* — Ah! That does credit to your judgment. Of course, they *redressed* you.

" *Cusick.*—Guess not—got de same clothes on yet. Dey was mitey cibbil, and said a good deal about de negro an' all dat, an' drew up a ' *card* ' for me to publish, an' charged me ten dollars for it, an' I hadn't it, and dat's de reason I guess dat it didn't go in.

" *Int.*—You was pretty well *car'd* already, I should imagine.

" *Cusick.*—Yes, bossy, but I didn' *car'*. for dat. I wanted to git damages, and dat's what I tole de clerk. An' he says, says he, ' I'll gub you damages ;' and wid dat he roll me down de steps ob de press-room, an' de pressman dipped me in de ink troff, and de boys lafft, and I crawled out like a *fly* out ob a molasses jug. And dey said ' *Shoo fly !*' when I disappeared roun' de corner.

" *Int.* — Having inked you I should have struck you off—taken an impression.

" *Cusick.*—Same ting ; dey struck my name off deir proscription list, and jus' den when I was gwine roun' de corner to go home, a ash-man hove his ash barrel, and I got de whole table o' contents all over ; an' de ashes stuck to de ink, and de ink stuck to de mortar, and de mortar stuck to my clothes, an' I yelled out:— 'Let me be!' and came over h'yar to take up a prescription.

"*Int.* — Well, Cusick, give us a jig and we'll see what can be done for you; and then Juniper Brignoll will sing us his latest song about

THE GOOD OLD NEW YORK GENTLEMAN.

" Come listen friends and neighbours, while a story I relate,
Of a hale and hearty gentleman well-known in every state ;
A man of weight and influence among the rich and great,
Who owns within Manhattan's bounds a flourishing estate—
 This natty New York gentleman, all of the modern time !

" He was the special favourite of all, I've heard it said,
Who lived within his range, and on all sides his favours shed ;
And stocks would rise and stocks would fall whene'er he'd
 shake his head,
While in his frown there lurked a spell made thousands quake
 with dread,
And yet was so awfully fraternal and condescending to those
 who nary read,
 This natty New York gentleman, all of the modern time !

" He loved good living, and could drink of lager beer a tun,

And meet him when you would, 'tis said, was running o'er with fun,

And oft upon the stump his eloquence our ears would stun,

Until the fight waxed fierce and hot, and by the exercise of his peculiar powers of persuasion, he had compelled his enemies to run—

    This natty New York gentlemen, all of the modern time !

" He knew the winning cards by heart, and when in a tight place

Could save himself and fill his purse by coppering on the ace ;

He knew the winning horses, too, and won at every race,

And wasn't in the least afraid a pistol's mouth to face.

And if anybody thought of arresting him for any of his little peccadilloes the probability is that before they caught him they'd have a most exciting chase—

    This natty New York gentleman, all of the modern time !

" He owned a railroad to himself, and eke a silver mine,

And 'mid the toppiest of the *ton* on evenings used to shine,

Besides a few score lots or so on the city's boundary line,

And if he hadn't sold them he'd have had them still, and his elegant establishment, and his dogs and his horses and his troops of friends, and a great many other things too numerous to mention, I opine—

    This natty New York gentleman, all of the modern time !

But every dog must have his day, and so it chanced at
    last

This good old soul, whose only fault was that he lived too
    fast,

Himself was forced to feel the blight of stern misfortune's
    blast ;

He rallied, but alas! for him the fatal die was cast.

He gave up his wines and his hounds, and his horses, his little
    parties, his excursions, his yachts and his youthful frivolities
    and into oblivion passed—

    This natty New York gentleman, all of the modern time!

Of course all know that this song is
not original, but a parody on " The Fine Old
English Gentleman," which has frequently been
treated to the same indignity at home. Very
much of early American verses and music was
at first thus obtained, but of late years a
change has taken place, and the cultivation of
their talents has resulted in the production of
songs which would do credit to any composer
or author. So rapid in fact has been the improvement in arts and sciences, and so generally
are native authors and composers appre-
ciated, that those who knew the literature

of America in all its branches twenty years ago would scarcely imagine how rich it has now become.

All being intensely fond of music, they are certain to become skilled in it, and their progress in poetry is evinced by the works of such new writers as are almost monthly startling Europeans by their force and originality.

I remember being present in a Western theatre when the celebrated comedienne and vocalist, Emily Thorne, played the part of Pocahontas, in the burlesque of that name, it being the first time that such an entertainment had been produced in that town. It was really ludicrous to watch the expressions of the audience, for they appeared as if undecided whether to laugh or cry. Either way, I believe, the tables might have been turned by a person bold enough to set the example.

Puns were specimens of wit with which, at that time, they were not very familiar, and although the curtain went down, leaving the spectators delighted with the music, all were puzzled to death at what conclusion to arrive in reference to the incidents and dialogue of Mr. Brougham's extremely clever and now very popular production. But a few short years have wrought a wonderful change, and the best productions of the Strand find their way to the New World in a marvellously short space of time.

Since I have been residing in this neighbourhood, there has been a most apparent increase in the value of land. This may be caused by the proposed carrying of a new line of railroad through the neighbourhood connecting Chicago with the Ohio river, which would confer many additional advantages on this part of the country.

The result is that many, particularly those of the poorer class, are disposing of their homesteads, that they may push off to the vast Uplands of Kanzas, Nebraska, and Iowa, which promise at no distant date to be the great pastoral region of the West.

Having visited that wonderful section of country, and traversed a considerable part of it, I cannot fail to commend such a course; for I sincerely wish this haven for husbandman and stock-raiser were better known, and more easy of access to our surplus home population.

The seasons here are not marked by such excessive changes of temperature as are peculiarly characteristic of the more eastern portion of the continent; and the country is well watered, has a fruitful soil, produces naturally abundance of nutritious grasses—its pleasant rolling surface presenting a great contrast to the vast steppe-like flats of Indiana and Illinois; for these dips, as they are frequently designated, afford a great natural advantage—shelter for homestead or farmyard from Winter winds.

Conversing with several of these intending emigrants, a characteristic which had struck me previously as eminently American was recalled, namely, their total want of love for any particular locality. This land may be too new to produce these feelings; for, of course excepting in the Eastern States, no properties can be found that have been in the hands of the same family through successive generations.

These sojourners, consequently, speak not a word of regret for the home they are leaving; but only anticipate the improvement in their worldly condition in the place they have selected as their future residence.

Still these people are intensely patriotic, and will take fire at the smallest imaginary insult offered to their nationality, thus evincing a love of country entirely peculiar in its nature, for it is not inspired by the thought that it contains their birthplace or ancestral homes. Yet the American is without an equal for cultivating and settling a new country. The peculiarities that I have enumerated as eminently qualifying him for the life of a soldier, are also those that are most requisite to the immigrant. For weeks and weeks, with their faces turned to the setting sun, these people will push onwards, ready to combat with all adversity, never discouraged or disheartened, relying on their courage and strength for protection, and on their endurance and resolution for the successful accomplishment of any object they propose. I bid them farewell on my departure for home.

I could not help wishing that their future life might be gilded with as much prosperity as the landscape that surrounded us was with the golden rays of the declining sun; and doubtless such will be the case, for the future home of their adoption possesses such numerous natural advantages that only a few years may pass before it is acknowledged as the most prosperous part of the great Republic.

Scandal, as already mentioned, is always abundant where facilities are granted for obtaining divorces, and the latter are so numerous here that they are discussed as every-day affairs. One of these stories, illustrating the occasional rivalries of man and wife, has just cropped up, and as it excites more than usual attention, either from its possessing a more than usually comic, or more than usually tragic element, I shall relate it.

"The people of the region round about are all agog, and decidedly conversationally disposed, over the conduct of a foreigner who has been arrested on the charge of bigamy. In regard to the event, the telegragh remitting the information informs us that he was first known hereabouts when he started a weekly newspaper, which soon, however, burst up.

"He became acquainted with Miss Liston, of this city, and soon married her. Not long afterwards he quitted the neighbourhood, and then his new-made wife lost all confidence in him, and proceeded to take legal measures for his capture.

"She and her father appeared before a magistrate and swore out a warrant against him for bigamy, believing that when he married Miss Liston he had a wife in Brooklyn. The warrant was placed in the hands of the proper officers, but before they had time to serve it, the absentee appeared at his bride's residence and explained everything satisfactorily, to her, at least, and made her a present of a beautiful watch and chain.

"The next morning the two appeared before the magistrate who issued the warrant, and had it nullified. The next morning the returned husband published a card in the public papers, assigning reasons for his sudden disappearance, and also giving out that he had received a letter from the old country announcing that he and his three sisters had fallen heirs to seventy-five thousand dollars. His young wife swallowed it, but not the father. He could not be hood-winked.

"He made a trip to Brooklyn, and there ascertained that in 1861 his daughter's husband married a little girl, aged fourteen years, in that city, and after fleecing her father out of nearly all the money he had, deserted his wife and fled to the South, where, during the war, he took up arms on the Confederate side. In the meantime, he married a beautiful girl there, who died soon afterwards.

"Leaving the South, he came North, and in October married Miss Liston. This last news reaching the ears of his Brooklyn wife, she hastened to obtain a divorce, not caring to prosecute for bigamy. She succeeded; but that does not save this Lothario from answering to the charge of bigamy, which charge is vigorously pushed by Miss Liston's father, though up to ten o'clock this morning the daughter was not aware of that fact.

"Through the same medium the following particulars were received:

"The foreigner arrested here on a charge of bigamy, was this morning examined before the Recorder. He was rather flashily attired in a black velvet coat, white vest, and drab pants. He wore side whiskers and a heavy moustache.

"As he sat down, his third wife, Miss Liston, took a chair beside him. She was attired in a straw-coloured walking suit, and wore a heavy gold watch and chain and other ornaments.

"About six feet away sat the first wife. She was dressed in a dark drab travelling suit with fashionable jockey. As the prisoner entered the dock, he gave one quick glance at her, and that was all. She, on the contrary, gazed earnestly and steadily at him, and at times smiled.

"Presently his counsel whispered:

"'Have you ever seen her before?'

" He replied :

" ' No, never."

" The counsel for the prosecution next whispered to her :

" ' Have you ever seen him before ?"

" She replied :

" ' Well, I rather kalkerlate I have,' and still kept gazing at him, he at all times avoiding her glance.

" The first wife was the first witness. As she ascended the stand it was apparent that she meant business. The counsel for the prosecution, after she had kissed the book, said :

" ' Look at that man ; have you seen him before ?"

" Witness—' Yes, sir, I have. My parents resided in New York. He left me in 1862, but I ran foul of him again in December last. He recognized me, but I would not recognize him. I was married to him in December, 1861. We lived together as man and wife until March 28th, 1862, at 50, Lispenard Street. I stayed there two or three months after he left me; I have had no communication with him since. He is the man I married, I think. I'm not mistaken. I am positive.'

" Cross-examined :—

" ' I first saw him at Broadway; he was alone. I can't tell the month or day; I never saw or heard of him before that time; I dare say we were married in two months after; he gave recommendations to my parents; they now live in Second Avenue; my father is in Indiana; been there eight or ten days; I have never seen the clergyman who married us since; we never kept house; he hadn't money enough to keep house with. [Laughter.] I had to pay out money to get his boots repaired. [Great laughter.] I got the money from my mother.

" ' I'm married again; never had any children; I was between fourteen and fifteen years of age when I married the prisoner; my parents told me to say sixteen, and I did. [Laughter.] He was in the Union army when I married him; toward the last he belonged

to what was called " The Lost Children." '
[Great laughter.]

"Counsel for the prosecution—'He's among
that class now, ain't he?' [Laughter.]

" Witness—'I should say so.' [Laughter.]

" Witness—'I have been married twice since
he left me; first time the day after I got a
divorce from him. I've got three husbands
now, and all living. [Witness and audience
laughing.] I'm living with my third husband.
He is a carpenter. I got a separation bill
from my second husband.'

" Witness was further examined by the defence, in order, if possible to find some flaw
in her testimony. She answered all the ques-
tions in a very straightforwad and unhesi-
tating manner. The pith of the evidence is
given in a statement which she made to the
reporter, after dinner.

" The first wife's statement is as follows :—

" 'I was forced to marry by my father. The
prisoner told him he had wronged me, when
my father said I must marry him or go to the

House of Refuge. I was young then, and didn't know as much as I do now. His story to my father was a wilful lie, but I married him because I did not wish to go to the House of Refuge. After I married him I avoided him all I could, and every time I saw him coming I would leave the house. One time I was gone seven days, and no one knew where I was.

" ' Finally he enlisted, and sent a letter to me by a revenue officer, saying that he knew I did not love him, and he was going to leave me for ever. Why, when I married him, my father had to pay the dominie. Oh, I'm so glad I got rid of that fellow! I don't want him to be sent to Sing Sing on my account. The world is wide enough for both of us. He never gave me one cent from the time he married me till he left me. He told me one day he would sell his sword and get me a pair of shoes, but he didn't.

" I'm happy now; I've got a good husband, and I love him. I wish they would call my mother up here. She would identify that chap right away.'

" A further examination of the case has been postponed until Tuesday, June 20th, at 10 a.m."

The above narrative, which certainly contains plenty of fun, shows in what an un-English state the laws, in reference to marriage, are in some of the Western States. The thorough business-manner in which the lady argues her case, and submits to cross-examination, proves that she is a person of no ordinary strength of mind, and perfectly capable of occupying the place that womans' rights advocates wish to confer on the gentler sex.

Although she, however, may be accepted as a capital type of a certain class of American females, I am happy to say that such are very much in the minority, even in that go-a-head country—a blessing that the sterner sex should not regard lightly.

Circumstances of a private nature now occurred at home which called for my immediate return to England, and it became imperative for me to part with my kennel, horses, &c.

On the day fixed for the sale, which was no-
tified to the public through the medium of the
Press, a large number of persons assembled,
and although purchasers were numerous, nearly
all my favourites went into the hands of acquaintances, and at prices that far exceeded
my expectations. In fact, one brace of setters
were knocked down to the purchaser at an
amount that would surprise even Mr. Garth in
his annual sales of pointers.

Although, therefore, I knew the pets had obtained good homes, it was not without regret
that I saw the horses I had ridden in many
a long journey and hard run, or the dogs I
had spent such happy days behind, and over
which I had killed so much game, led off by
their new owners. In youth, I loved animals,
and now, in mature age, my affection for them
has not diminished, for experience has taught
me how sincere is their devotion, how un-
selfish their affection.

The days before leaving were devoted to
leave-taking, and the earnest "God speed you!'
that many, both poor and rich, pronounced as

I bade them farewell, will never be forgotten as long as memory has the power to recall any of the numerous happy days spent upon a Prairie Farm and among Prairie Folk.

THE END.

LONDON: PRINTED BY A. SCHULZE, 13, POLAND STREET.